Gold Digger

Laura E Simms

Copyright 2013 Laura Elizabeth Simms

For Nathan

17 years, my friend. Can you believe it?

The man with the heart of gold. The man whose knowledge of war and history, dwarfs even my old history teacher, and I didn't think that was possible.

We've been through our rough times, but we weathered the storms. I know you're there, if I need you at any point.

Don't ever change for anyone.

You are unique. You have stuck with me through thick and thin.

I just want you to know though, there's not a day goes by, when I regret sitting under that table with you, on a Friday evening in October 1996.

You tell me you don't remember. That doesn't surprise me. But I do and believe me it's true.

The simplest things can be life-changing.

To Sara

I used to think, you didn't want to be in my head or in my dreams, but now I'm not sure, I want to be in yours.

This is the idea you gave me, though I'm not sure you intended it to be written this way, but we shall see.

Glossary and Definitions

The term "Gold Digger" is a slang phrase used to describe a greedy person. This is typically a woman and has become a stereotype. The modus operandi is to date and marry a wealthy person, with the sole intention of exploiting their fortune.

Prologue

Mid July 2043

She wrote a note, and then crossed it out again. The silver Parker pen, in her hand trembled.

Her advertisement had been answered, with several applications.

A few looked promising. But this posed a problem. A decision had to be made.

There were so many candidates that might fit, though not perfectly.

She dropped half of the application forms, on the floor with a loud slithering sound.

"Fuck!"

There was a knock on the door, and he came in. Her "guardian angel," so to speak.

No, they weren't lovers. Not now at least. It had been a teenage crush, but that was all, it had ever been.

He was unavailable now anyway. That might not have stopped most people, but it stopped her.

"Let me do it" he said patiently.

"I'm perfectly capable of..."

"But you're not though are you?" he said gently.

She didn't take offence. He hadn't meant it to be. He bent down, and gathered the papers together.

"Still going ahead then?" he asked, glancing down.

"Yep" she replied.

"Don't start" she added wearily, before he could interrupt.

"I wasn't going to. There would be no point"

The sigh in his voice, was evident. They had obviously had this argument many times before, whatever it was about. She moved away from the desk and gestured.

"What?" he looked confused.

"I thought you might have needed something. You came in"

"I heard you drop all that shit" he said carefully.

"Right"

The tone that answered was dull. He knew he needed to cheer her up, or he would not get another civil word, out of her that day.

"Cup of tea?" he asked.

"It's nearly time for your medication"

"I better had then, and a piece of cake or something"

"You need more than cake. You'll throw up. You know they erode your stomach lining, if you don't eat first. Did you go to the doctor?"

"Yes why?"

"I take it, you had your liver and kidney function tests"

"Yeah they're fine. Stop worrying"

"I'll get your lunch then"

She was barely back at her project, for 10 minutes before he was back carrying a plateful of food.

She had to admit, it looked good. He put down the cup.

"I'll leave you to it then" he said.

"I'm listening to music, if need me"

"That pop rubbish?"

He stuck his tongue out, and she grinned. He moved towards the door, and reached for the handle.

"Wayne?"

He looked back.

"Thanks" she said.

"What are friends for?"

"Listen. When are you going back?"

"Why? Am I outstaying my welcome?"

He looked worried, but winked.

"No. I'm just curious" she grinned.

"Well, things still aren't going too well, between me and..."

"Say no more. Stay as long as you like"

She watched thoughtfully as he exited.

She circled one set of information, with her red pen. Then she pulled her laptop towards her.

She loaded the Internet browser, and in a pecking motion, typed a query into Google.

The search was fast. Tenths of seconds if that. This sort of search, should be illegal and probably was.

The best spying weapons, were the Internet and the phone book. People didn't seem to realize this, however.

Look in the phone book, and not only could you find someone's name, but also their address and landline phone number.

A quick search of Facebook, brought up the profile she was looking for.

The person's profile page, wasn't privacy protected.

She found all the information, within seconds.

She logged into her own e-mail account, and sent a message.

Target Acquired
Gold Digger

The reply came back almost instantly.

Who?

See attached document.
CV.doc
Gold Digger

When?

Wait a few months
Let me get close
Gold Digger

Discussion of payment pending.

On completion. Not before. No negotiation.
Gold Digger

The stream of communication stopped. It was all arranged then.

She erased the computer's history, it would not do, to have that found, if the computer was found or searched.

She sat back, her fingers stiff, her energy zapped, but a huge smile on her face.

All she had to do was sit back, wait for things to go to hell, and then there would be a huge payday.

Chapter One

Three months later

Rose-Anna Rabin, would never forget this Saturday in late November, as long as she lived, and unless she played her cards right, that wouldn't be long.

Not that at this point, in proceedings she knew this, as she got ready for work. in front of her bedroom mirror.

She studied her reflection. She was 23 years old, and she looked at least ten years older.

It was worry she supposed, or the stress of holding down three jobs.

The most recent of which, was at the bank. She was also worried about Gabrielle.

She'd gone to the cinema with her, and Gabrielle had seemed distracted.

But she couldn't afford, to worry about that now. She was running late again.

She would figure out, what to do about Gabrielle later.

She wasn't sure, she'd be staying at the bank much longer.

It wasn't that it was beneath her. Far from it, but she was a cashier, treated like shit and generally trod upon.

She was thinking of reporting the manager, for sexual harassment.

His behaviour was something like, the cinema manager's treatment of Joan Trotter, in the prequel to Only Fools and Horses, Rock n Chips.

However, they were not now, in the 1960s and she didn't have to put up with it.

Her rights as a woman had changed.

Brushing herself down one last time, she descended the stairs. Her sister Elizabeth-Ellen, older than her by a year or two, sprawled on the sofa.

Rose-Anna hadn't heard the doorbell ring. Elizabeth-Ellen lived with her fiancé. She would marry him this coming February.

It was a little cheesy, to get married on Valentine's Day. Elizabeth-Ellen looked up at Rose-Anna's entrance.

"I'm going to need your measurements, and don't lie, Rose. If it doesn't fit tough shit, you're wearing it"

"Would I? Do I have to do it now? I'm late for work"

"Tomorrow's fine" her sister replied.

"And yes you would"

Rose-Anna grabbed her car keys from the table, kissed her mother goodbye, promised not to be late and left the house, pausing only to stick her tongue out, at her sister.

She didn't therefore, see Elizabeth-Ellen stick her middle finger up at her.

Not that she would have cared, if she had seen it.

Her car was parked in the garage, round the block rather than in the driveway.

There were often too many cars parked, to be able to get a space, so it was housed in the garage.

It was quite a long walk, but Rose-Anna liked fresh air. She breathed deeply.

There was no one else around. She reached the garage, and opened the door.

It was pitch black in there. She was feeling for the light switch, when a sound made her jump.

"Hello?" she called.

There shouldn't be anyone there. No answer.

She shook herself mentally. Perhaps it was an animal, knocking something over. It wasn't necessarily anything sinister.

She went back, to looking for the light switch again, but stopped as there was a rattle.

"Who's there?" she said, trying not to let her voice quiver.

No answer.

"This is ridiculous. Pull yourself together Rose" she told herself sternly.

Suddenly the garage filled with light. Not because she'd finally located, the damn light switch, but because there was a torch beam, shining in her eyes.

She blinked and tried to shield her eyes, but with little success.

She was still blinded. All she could see, were shadows.

"Who are you?" she asked.

No answer. She shuddered slightly.

She had to admit it now; she was starting to get nervous.

"What do you want?" she said.

"Always the same questions" a voice hissed in her ear.

She jumped violently.

"Careful"

"Not very original are they?"

"Nope. It's so boring"

"Who are you? What do you want?" one of them mimicked.

Rose-Anna could feel a sense of danger, but she couldn't quite explain why.

She just knew, she needed to be careful.

"What do you want?" she asked again.

Would they answer this time?

"It depends. Are you Rose-Anna Rabin?"

Rose-Anna thought for a second. She hated the name Rose-Anna, preferring just plain "Rose."

She could say no, announce that she was Elizabeth-Ellen.

She would get away, but they wouldn't go away. They would just wait around, and ambush "Lizzie."

Could she allow this to happen? Lizzie was fucking annoying, but she was her sister.

Blood was thicker than water, and all that shit.

"So are you?" the voice hissed again.

"Y...Yes" she stammered, wondering what would come; now she'd admitted this.

"You need to come with us"

"Come with you where? Why? What if I refuse?"

"You'll see when we get there. We just want to talk to you that's all, and if you don't come quietly, we'll have to make you"

"Talk to me here" she said.

"Oh we can't do that. Too much chance of interruptions"

She gulped. What was that supposed to mean? Interrupt what exactly?

Dark scenes began to play in her head. An involuntary shudder ran through her.

He looked down, and started fingering his belt. She followed his gaze, and her blood ran cold. There was a gun sticking out of that belt.

"That's..." her voice came out hoarse.

She cleared her throat and tried again.

"That's not loaded is it?"

"That's for us to know, and for you to find out"

"I'm supposed to be going to work"

"Not today you're not"

"But..."

"I suggest, if you like your brain and guts where they are, you come with us"

His tone was chillingly casual, conversational even.

"You could tell whoever you work for, you couldn't find me"

Her tone was begging now. She hated the sound of it.

"Sorry, no can do"

His tone did sound vaguely apologetic. She had been afraid, that this would be the case.

"Can't you shut her up? We're on a schedule, and she's getting on my nerves" the other voice complained.

Rose-Anna knew she should scream. It would attract an audience, but no sooner had the thought occurred, than they cut this off.

She suddenly tasted leather. She bit down hard with her teeth. He cursed loudly, but removed his hand.

She tried to twist out of his grip. But he simply tightened his own.

This was a simple strategy. He waited for her to exhaust herself. It didn't take very long.

"Finished?" he enquired.

She nodded.

"Good because we have stuff to do. Guess we're doing this the hard way then" he commented.

"Please, you don't have to do this. You really don't"

"If it was up to me, we wouldn't. But we have orders. If I were you, I'd be a good girl, and do as you're told"

Before she knew what had happened, it had gone dark and she could barely breathe.

She felt herself, being lifted off her feet and carried. Her world appeared to have tipped upside down. She couldn't fight anymore.

Chapter Two

Rose-Anna couldn't deny it now. She was terrified. She was in deep, deep trouble.

One question resounded in her numbed brain, over and over and over again.

That question was why? The frustrated scream of it, echoed in her head.

Her bladder was in danger of voiding. She was determined not to do this, it would just be so embarrassing.

She had been in here, for what felt like hours. They were still moving.

She could feel this, the floor was rumbling and every so often, she would lose her balance, for no apparent reason.

Her mind was going at one hundred miles an hour, which wasn't necessarily a good thing.

What could they possibly want with her? Mistaken identity?

No they'd called her. by her proper given hideous Christian name.

She couldn't understand why, she would become a target. She was a lowly cashier, in terms of the bank anyway.

She wanted to scream, that she was a nobody, a Nobody.

Following orders they'd said, whose orders?

They kept stopping, and she'd think they were wherever they were going, but they'd move off again.

If she did, whatever they needed her to do, would they set her free, she sincerely hoped so, but fiercely doubted it.

She could describe things about them, maybe not what they looked like, but accents at least.

She was now dangerous to them, if she were kept alive after the business, whatever it was, had been concluded.

No. She had to think positively. She would be fine. She had to be.

She should have been in the bank by now. She would be missed, and if she didn't return, she would be reported missing.

Her stomach dropped like a stone. They would use her full name. Everyone would know what it was.

But then she shook herself. It wouldn't matter what they called her, as long as she was around long enough, for them to call her something.

Eventually though, the vehicle she was travelling in came to a permanent standstill.

She waited to see what would happen next.

The floor rocked, as extra weight was added.

"Out!" the now familiar voice barked.

Rose-Anna tried to obey, but her legs were weak now. She stumbled slightly.

"Oh for fuck's sake" a far more threatening voice growled.

She felt like she was flying, as she was swept off her feet.

She was sat in someone's arms, and bounced with each step.

She tried to count the seconds or minutes, but soon lost count.

The temperature kept dropping lower and lower. Perhaps they were going underground.

The thought scared her. As a child, she got stuck underground, exploring a cave and had had to be rescued.

The fact she was underground now. was just supposition however.

She was suddenly back on firm ground. She thought she could hear a clink or rattle.

But maybe she had imagined it.

The clang of the metal door, as it closed echoed in her ears.

She was presumably alone now. She tried to move her hand, but found it wouldn't extend very far.

She quickly worked out why. She was chained to the wall. She felt the first salty tears, beginning to fall.

Chapter Three

The woman in the wheelchair, closed the laptop rather abruptly.

"So what exactly took you so long?" she demanded.

"She was a little difficult"

"Difficult? You're far stronger than her. Are you men or mice?"

"Men of course"

"Are you sure, because I just don't see it. How exactly did you subdue her?"

"She's fine. Perfectly alert"

"Good. She needs to be. We'll need her in a while"

"Not going to plan then?"

"Of course it isn't. What have you got for brains? Shit?"

"She won't co-operate with you"

"Oh she will trust me. We don't need her, we need what she can provide" the woman said cryptically.

The thug looked confused.

"I don't get it"

"You're not supposed to. Tell Wayne, I want him"

Some five minutes later, a man well over 6 feet tall walked in.

The first thing you noticed about this man, was the eyes. Icebergs cowered in their presence.

They were the clearest blue ever witnessed, with just a hint of grey in a ring, round the edges.

The man looked intimidating, but he possessed the gentlest of natures.

He had been trying to persuade her, not to go ahead with a plan, they had conceived one drunken evening.

Wayne had at that point, lost his job, but he had since found another.

He knew he would lose this one, if the plot were discovered.

The plan had originally been suggested in jest. He was here now, only because he wanted, to see the woman in the wheelchair, came to no harm.

She loved him in a platonic way for this. They had known each other, since the dawn of time, or so it felt sometimes.

"What?" he asked, his tone sulky.

"I was reading"

"Anything interesting?"

"The legend of Oedipus"

"You've read that a thousand times, to my knowledge"

"Well I like it"

"Let me refresh my memory here. It's about the king of Thebes, and his wife the queen, who abandons their child, because of a prophecy that says he'll kill his father, and marry his mother. He is adopted by a shepherd and his wife, and nurtured until he grows up. The King is then murdered, and the queen marries again and has more children, but it turns out that he has in fact. done as the prophecy says, killed his father and married his mother"

"In simple terms yes"

"So he blinds himself as penance"

"That's the one"

"Wayne, the only decent part of that story, is the evil uncle, what's his name Creon, burying Oedipus's daughter Antigone, therefore Creon's own niece in a wall, he commits nieceicide, or whatever the fuck the term is. He killed his niece anyway, the sick bastard. Oh and the other jolly thing is, Queen Jocasta hanging herself. I couldn't stand her."

"You're a cheerful soul. I think it's just murder or genocide. Though I know, if you kill your brother or sister it's fratricide. Not sure they are that specific, about nieces or nephews" Wayne commented.

"Wayne, that play is dull as ditchwater"

"It's a tragedy, what do you expect?"

"Something original. I'm sorry, it's not a subject, that I should be teasing about. It's serious"

"The play gives you the creeps, always has done. You can't fool me Gabby. Sophocles is a legend himself though"

"If you say so. Remind me, what your objection to this plan is"

"It's unnecessary"

"Wayne they did you over. You need to learn, to stand up for yourself"

"There has to be another way. What's her name, is down there, probably scared out of her mind. Not to mention innocent. It's not her fault. She'll pay a price, and it isn't even her debt"

"Rose. Her name is Rose. Even if I wanted to change my mind, which I don't by the way. It's done. We can't let her go. She'll blab"

"What could she possibly say? She was taken hostage this morning, by two guys. She's had a bag over her head, for the best part of 5 hours. She hasn't seen you. You're the only one, she can identify"

"No it's gone too far. It went too far, the second it came into my head. You can still get out though Way.

"Nope. If you go down, I do too"

"But what about...?"

"Let me worry about that. As far as they know, I'm away on business. Hey, you should keep warm. You're shivering. You'll have consequences you don't want"

"Wayne stop fussing. I'm fine"

"Listen, all your guilty of, is trying to help a friend and I appreciate it. You didn't actually kidnap her, the guys did that, and if they implicate you, deny it"

"The poor little disabled woman, always victimised?"

"You see being in that thing, does have its compensations"

"Very limited ones"

"Yeah, but some. Listen, I'm going to bed, but I can fetch you a bottle of wine. You need to loosen up, before your muscles set"

"Alcohol doesn't solve it Wayne"

"If only. It'll loosen you up though"

"Wayne, are you coming onto me?"

Her tone was light and teasing.

He pointed to the wedding finger of his left hand, where the simple gold band, encircled and glinted when it caught the light, the sobering reminder.

This was his standard response, to any innuendo. They knew each other too well, to take the conversation any further, or indeed seriously.

"Night Wayne"

"Night Gabby"

After he'd gone she reflected. She wouldn't have got into this mess, if she wasn't fiercely loyal to Wayne.

Did she feel guilty, that Rose-Anna was in the cellar downstairs? Of course, she wasn't a monster.

Sighing deeply, she wheeled herself into the adapted room, which housed her bed.

She languidly transferred herself. Grunting slightly, as she stood, however briefly, upon the weakening ankles that would one day, simply refuse to bear her weight any longer.

The money would pay for her care. It was as simple as that. She might have to get in a live in nurse, eventually.

The doctors had assured her, that her condition would neither degenerate nor improve, but time was her enemy.

As she got older, her body would succumb as everyone's would, to age.

Her joints and muscles, which already took a punishing amount of strain, would not be up to the job.

Her ankle joints, had been protesting since the age of 9 and a half, one day walking across the sports field, she had been pitched off her crutches.

Understanding had dawned then, on the nine year old that life would never be the same again.

Over the next few years, the joints had deteriorated to the point that she fell frequently, often hitting her head.

The doctors warned, that if she hit her head, with that much force again, her already damaged brain, would become even more so.

Eventually, she would hit her head so hard, she would go into a coma, and may not wake up from it.

So by the age of just 10, her terrified parents insisted, she remain wheelchair-bound.

Was what she was doing to Rose, morally or even remotely right?

No. In fact, she sometimes wished that the doctors' darkest predictions, had come true.

She had to look in the mirror, and see a body that by the age of 26, had already more than half-broken, for the simple reason, it had never worked properly.

But up until today, she had been able to accept this. But now she wasn't so sure.

She didn't recognise the person, staring back at her out of the mirror.

Chapter Four

Sunday 5:30pm

Rose-Anna wasn't sure, how much time had passed. She had tried sleeping, but had not slept, for more than an hour. She tried counting imaginary sheep.

They had given her a mattress, to sleep on and it doubled for some kind of seat, maybe not a comfortable one, but better than the cold, hard stone floor.

"Rose" read crime novels, but they didn't adequately explain, how fucking boring being a hostage, actually was.

Because that was what she was, wasn't it? No one had actually said the word, but it was obvious now she thought about it.

The only explanation was, that her part whatever that was, hadn't taken place yet.

The phrase "borrowed time" sprang to mind.

"Think positive. They still need you, which for the time being, means you'll stay alive" she told herself sternly.

"Yeah and after?" a whining voice in her brain asked.

"We cross that bridge, when we come to it" the first voice said firmly.

She wished she could have some human contact, any would do even Lizzie's.

Lizzie, did her family know yet? Were they searching for her?

The only time she'd had company, was when they brought in food, and let her empty her bulging bladder.

She crossed her legs, as this thought occurred. She needed to empty it again.

She had managed to avoid, wetting herself yesterday, she would do so again.

The sound of the door opening, made her jump and scramble to find her feet.

The man who came in, was carrying her evening meal on a tray. On the tin tray, was a folded newspaper.

He said nothing, but bent and freed her hands. She dropped rapidly to all fours, and crawled as swiftly as possible. She only just made it, to the bucket in time.

Once back in position, she wolfed down the food, barely pausing to chew, before swallowing.

Once this was done, she held out her hands, so he could put the restraints back in place.

This was the routine, they had followed yesterday.

The man shook his head, and pointed to the newspaper.

"You want me to read it?"

He nodded.

Sighing deeply, she unfolded the newspaper. Her eyes travelled down the page, and widened.

There was a photograph, right next to the by-line. She had always thought, that photo was hideous.

She'd wanted to destroy it, 5 seconds after it was taken. There had to be better ones, they could have used.

It was one of her, when she was going to a fancy dress party, last Halloween.

She had decided to go, as a vampire. She thoroughly regretted that decision now.

She hadn't thought for one second, that the photograph would be on public display.

The journalist who wrote the story, was the crime correspondent.

There wasn't much information, to report at the moment, just rumours.

HAVE YOU SEEN THIS WOMAN?

Employer issues £25,000 reward for information regarding the disappearance of employee.

Rose-Anna Rabin (23), disappeared from her home yesterday morning. Miss Rabin works at her local bank as a cashier.

She left for work, about 9:00 yesterday morning, but appears to have vanished en route.

Do you know what happened, to this young woman?

DI Ivor Gunn, who is investigating Rose-Anna's disappearance, issued the following statement.

"We are extremely concerned about the safety of Rose-Anna. She was meant to come home last night, and didn't. This is extremely out of character for her.

She has not made contact, and we would urge her to do so, if she is able to. If she is not able to, we would urge you to allow her to. If you are holding Rose-Anna against her will, for whatever reason, we urge you to make your agenda known.

We are open to negotiation. The safe return of Rose-Anna is paramount."

Rose-Anna gulped.

What did this mean for her now? Was the publicity, a good or a bad thing?

"They published my full name, but I don't like Rose-Anna. Everyone knows me as Rose"

It wasn't what she wanted to say, but she couldn't act, like she was scared. They couldn't know that, at any cost.

The man rolled his eyes. As if the silly bitch, was worrying about a name, not that she knew this yet, but she would soon have much more serious things, to worry about, than what name she had been reported missing under.

When he left, Rose-Anna felt the tears running down her cheeks again.

She couldn't wipe them away though. She seemed to be crying, an awful lot lately. It was so unlike her.

Her legs were already protesting. Depending which guard she got, depended what position she was tied back up in.

This one had tied her, to the supporting beam in the ceiling.

Her hands were above her head. It was excruciating and she would be in this position, for 12 hours if not longer.

If she wanted to change position at all, she had to crouch.

Chapter Five

Monday 8:30am

Heidi Rabin paced, as she had done, for most of the night hours and much of the previous day.

She reviewed the hours, since she'd last seen her youngest daughter.

She thought it might stay with her forever. Elizabeth-Ellen had stayed several hours, going through her wedding plans.

She was now panicking because her chief bridesmaid, was missing in action, as the Army would put it.

However, Heidi was getting ahead of herself again. She couldn't afford to do so.

Rose had been due back from work, and she hadn't come back.

At first, they hadn't been worried. Rose was a grown adult; she could meet a friend perhaps.

Time had moved on though, and they started to get worried.

Heidi first, admittedly. Eddie had always been less likely to panic.

He advised that they wait, before reacting drastically.

She hadn't liked this idea in the slightest, eventually though when Rose hadn't been seen, for well over 24 hours, he had picked up the phone himself, and reported her missing.

The Police had arrived promptly. They appeared to have sent the big guns.

CID had arrived in the form, of DI Ivor Gunn and DS Arthur Jobb.

They had listened most attentively, taken statements and made enquiries, even on a Sunday.

They had reported back. Rose hadn't gone to work on Saturday.

Her car wasn't in the garage, but apparently that meant nothing.

It may well have been disposed of. There had been a press conference.

Eddie had gone along, but he had not spoken at it.

The Police were now discussing a theory, that Rose had been kidnapped.

This thought terrified her. Since the idea had been pitched, her imagination had run wild.

Images crowded her head once again. Rose chained up like a dog, perhaps in the dark.

How Rose hated the dark, since the cave incident.

Rose covered in blood, cowering in the corner. They would be no friend to her.

Rose lying dead, broken bones and much worse things.

With difficulty, Heidi pulled her mind away. The Police also said, that judging by the state of the garage, if that was where the event in question had taken place, whatever that truly was, then Rose had gone down fighting.

This gave Heidi an odd sense of pride. Her daughter had been able to defend herself.

She had forced her attackers, to get creative.

DI Gunn had told them, that Rose would be safe, as long as the people holding her hostage, hadn't fulfilled their purpose.

But no matter, how hard she tried, she couldn't for the life of her, understand how her daughter could be mixed up in anything, that required abduction as a routine method of operation.

They had been informed, that if a ransom demand was to be made, it would be made within 72 hours, and then there would be hope. So far nothing.

Had the "purpose" been achieved? Was it already too late?

She had to pray, that it wasn't. She wasn't sure she could live, with the alternative.

She knew her husband was suffering, but he'd never admit it.

He had gone to work today, trying to be normal, she supposed.

She on the other hand, had called in sick. She wouldn't have been able to concentrate.

Lizzie had rung, presumably for news. She had had to admit, there was none.

Lizzie had gone through an interview, with the Police. She had been the last known person, other than her mother to see Rose, bar her possible kidnappers.

She claimed, she couldn't help them very much.

She was now whining, talking about the need, to find a fresh bridesmaid, as Rose had so inconsiderably gone missing.

Though she was somewhat excited, to think that her younger sister's disappearance, might get her wedding covered by magazines, such as Hello or OK!

Heidi had never before realized, just how superficial and shallow, Elizabeth-Ellen really was.

She barely knew where her feet, were automatically taking her.

But she found herself, sitting on Rose's bed, gazing round the room, as though ordered to memorise it.

It was the same shade of lilac, it had been since her daughter was 6 years old.

Rose may have added posters, as she went through her teenage years, but otherwise it remained unchanged.

She found an odd sense of comfort here, surrounded by her daughter's things.

It was as though, she'd just popped to the shop, and would return at any time.

Would Rose ever be in here again? Heidi knew there was as yet, no answer to that.

Chapter Six

Earlier on Monday morning

Rose-Anna had been woken, abruptly and unmercifully. The smart work clothes of Saturday, were disgustingly dirty, creased and stank to high heaven by now.

She had scrambled to find her feet. She wasn't being carried this time, if she was required to go anywhere. She would walk under her own steam.

They didn't speak to her, the two in the masks who came for her; just put the hooded, for want of a better word bag, over her head. She wasn't really sure, why they bothered.

If asked, she wouldn't be able, to give many details. She hated the fact, that they had laid a guiding hand on her, but what else could she expect.

They walked, for what felt like half an hour, but was probably only minutes.

She heard something scrape across the floor, and felt the chair against her.

Automatically, she sat in it. The cold sensation told her, she was once again restrained.

She tugged, and there was a horrible noise, of wooden legs being dragged across the room, the table.

A slithering sound, rubber travelling across the floor?

"Morning Rose"

The shock, of the familiar voice was electric, but it couldn't be, it just couldn't be.

"Gabrielle?" she stammered.

The hood was suddenly removed, and Rose-Anna blinked.

She waited for her eyes to adjust, and then looked up.

She had never seen a look so cruel, on Gabrielle Cullen's face, well on anyone's face.

It chilled her to the bone, this amusement.

"Should I have an eye patch, and be stroking a cat. I have the wheelchair after all. It's just like a Bond film isn't it?

Rose-Anna didn't respond immediately, but did some quick mental calculation, and fitted things together.

The realization made her mouth go dry, she felt like she'd swallowed her tongue, as she tried to find the words.

"It was you all along"

Why was her tongue, suddenly determined to jump out of her mouth?

I thought we were friends, but..." she tried again.

"But, but, but" Gabrielle mimicked her.

"And who on earth, said we were friends?"

"You had this planned all along, didn't you?"

"Now the dumb bitch gets it"

"When did you become so hard, bitter, cruel and twisted? When did you develop, a heart of stone?"

"Become? I'm a good actress Rose. I've always been like this."

Rose could see then, that if there had ever been anything human about Gabrielle, then it was gone now.

The older woman, seemed to reconsider her answer however.

"Eight months ago I had everything, and I lost it. My heart hasn't beat since. At least, not in the figurative sense. Ever since, I've been trying to get there, and not succeeding. It'll get better they said. Perhaps it's for the best. Time will heal. What the fuck do they know? It still feels, like someone drove a skewer, through my heart, and I'm still impaled upon it"

Her voice was so quiet, Rose-Anna almost didn't hear.

"What... Why am I here?"

"Because you're useful to me, at the moment"

"And when I'm not?"

"Do you really want me to answer that?"

No. She didn't did she?

"I think I can guess. And when do I stop being useful?"

"That depends"

"On?"

"That's for me to know. But by all means, see if you can't work it out"

"When you advertised, I'd just started working at the bank. I'd been there a few weeks. Oh God, you want the money. That friend of yours, who was area manager worked there, but he got fired. You knew what the security was, but now you don't. You need..."

"Keep going"

"You need someone who works there, to get you past the new security"

"Gold star"

"It won't work, they'll have activated the shutdown of my access, and they know I'm, I'm in your hands"

"They only suspect, you are doing an impression of Sooty, Sweep and Sue. But yes you're right. The shutdown takes 24 hours, the transfer takes 3, they activated it 19 hours ago, 5 hours to go and we'll have a clear 2 hours"

"What if I don't do it? You need my fingerprint and retina pattern, its individual and then the password"

"That can be arranged"

Gabrielle raised her hand, and Rose-Anna heard the sound of movement, behind her.

She was suddenly airborne, with the table dragging behind her.

She tried to struggle, but the grip that held her, stayed firm.

"Idiot" Gabrielle said.

Her hands were briefly free, and the handcuffs locked again.

She was suddenly on the table. Her hands were above her head, vice like.

She twisted, but there was no way, they were coming loose.

One of her fingers was further out, than the others. It had been deliberately positioned that way.

The thug produced a knife, and flicked the blade. It was an ugly thing with a serrated edge, at least 7 inches long.

He advanced on her, and she suddenly saw what was coming. She should have guessed really.

She couldn't help it, she started to squeal, like a pig about to be made into bacon.

They needed her fingerprints, they could just take them. They needed her retina patterns, what was to stop them taking that too.

She had sudden visions, of the physicist Leonardo Vetra at the start of Dan Brown's novel, Angels and Demons.

When his killer, supposedly from the legendary group the Illuminati, had needed to break a biometric password, he had simply removed, one of his victim's eyeballs.

She closed her eyes, and willed herself not to throw up. The knife hovered, dangerously close to her finger.

Surely they wouldn't actually do this, not without anesthetising her first.

The pain and shock would kill her, and surely they'd get a qualified surgeon to do it, not this butcher.

The blood loss and potential infection, was potentially catastrophic.

So much potential fatality, Gabrielle seemed to have thought this through though.

"Haven't you forgotten something?" Gabrielle's tone was exasperated.

The thug reached over, and extracted a syringe.

Rose-Anna went even paler.

She had an insane phobia of needles, syringes fell into that category. She couldn't explain why either.

No childhood incident, she could remember was to blame.

"Don't tense up. It hurts more, if you do" Gabrielle advised.

She should know, Rose-Anna supposed. She had had more needles in her life, than most hospitals stocked.

Fuck that though, he was going to take her finger and her eyeball.

Her automatic reaction was to writhe. Gabrielle sighed and muttered something.

It sounded like

"Fucking incompetence."

The thug put a firm hand, on her stomach. It was painful.

She wanted to kick him, but resisted the temptation. It would only lead, to trouble later. His hand went to the plunger.

"A little less, she'll be too stoned to do anything"

Gabrielle's tone hadn't softened, one little bit.

She gave the thug in her command, a look that would turn him to stone, if he didn't obey her.

The man holding Rose-Anna's life, in his hands scowled.

However, he followed instructions. The syringe was suddenly in her arm. All he had to do, was push it down.

She watched the clear liquid, go through the tube and begin its journey, into her body.

Irresistible waves began to take her. She could go to sleep, and when she woke up, it would be over.

She would be minus an eyeball and a finger, but did it really matter?

Everything was going black. Her eyelids fluttered almost closed, without being told.

Her brain suddenly caught up with itself. They were going to cut off her finger, and remove her eyeball.

NO! She couldn't let them do it. She couldn't pass out. But maybe it was the easy option.

She had just seconds, to make a decision. Her heart rate accelerated.

Did she give in, and do as they asked, or did she stick to her principles?

The thoughts raced through her mind, in a quarter of a second, calculating.

Somehow, she managed to swim up from the depths, and find the will to speak, from the edge of darkness, nearly engulfing her.

"OK, OK. I give up. You win, I'll do it" her voice sounded slurred, even to her own ears.

"What did you say?" Gabrielle said.

"I said I'd do it. Just don't let him stick any more of that stuff in me. Please to God, don't let him do that" she repeated herself, trying to speak clearly.

Gabrielle nodded, and suddenly the pressure was off her.

The needle had vanished from her arm. Her hand was free. She stared at it. Her finger was still attached to it.

She had double vision, but this started to clear, once she shook her head.

She found her feet, though she was visibly shaking. There were tear tracks, streaking her cheeks. She recognised her feelings, as the beginnings of shame.

Though she couldn't understand why. It would be enough, to make someone twice her age; even some grown men, shit themselves.

The small amount of make-up she wore, just mascara made black marks, as it smudged.

She wiped them away angrily. The back of her hand came away black.

She was a little annoyed, (a) that the tears had fallen at all and (b) because the mascara, had been advertised as waterproof and obviously wasn't.

But that was trivial. She needed to get out of here.

She still felt drunk. She suspected even the small amount of drug, whatever it was in her system, would linger for a while.

She tried to guess what it was, but soon gave up. She had started to go under, so fast.

Gabrielle pushed the laptop towards her. Rose-Anna's legs felt like water, but somehow she made it to the desk.

She dropped to her knees, it was safer, she was already on the floor should she, not be able to support her own weight.

She touched the keys. The computer hummed to her touch.

She touched her finger to the screen. A few seconds later, she lined up her eye.

She was barely breathing, but this part of the operation, seemed to have been accepted, without a hitch.

She typed in the final password.

"How much do you want?"

Her tone was dull. Her speech still slurred a little.

"I'll do that bit"

Gabrielle reached for the laptop, and Rose-Anna pushed it, to within her reach.

Gabrielle pressed keys, presumably the numbers. She weakly shoved it, and Rose-Anna took it back.

The screen was flashing, asking for the authorisation code.

Sighing deeply, she typed in the requested code, and pressed the "Enter" key.

The coloured squares counted down, accepting the transaction.

"Thank you" Gabrielle said.

"You didn't give me a choice" Rose-Anna pointed out.

"Is that it?" she asked.

"Not quite" Gabrielle replied.

Chapter Seven

DI Ivor Gunn and DS Arthur Jobb, were getting nowhere in the search, for Rose-Anna Rabin.

Her image, the most recent one smiled down, from the whiteboard.

Notes spread out like spiders, confused and making no sense.

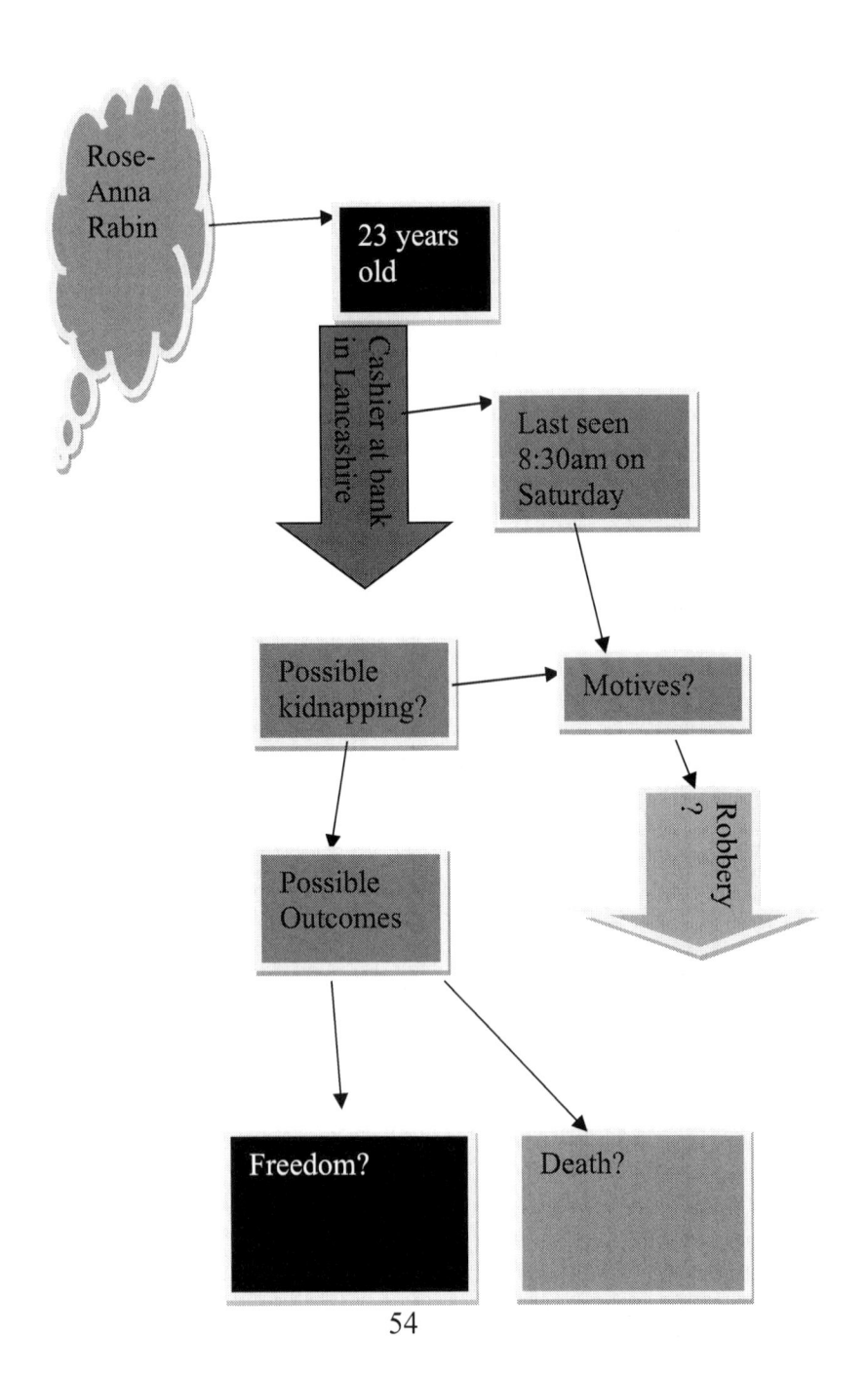

```
                    ┌──────────────┐
  Rose-       →     │ 23 years old │
  Anna              └──────┬───────┘
  Rabin                    │ Cashier at bank in Lancashire
                           │              ┌──────────────────┐
                           │         →    │ Last seen 8:30am │
                           │              │ on Saturday      │
                           ↓              └────────┬─────────┘
                  ┌──────────────┐                 │
                  │ Possible     │  →    ┌─────────▼──┐
                  │ kidnapping?  │       │ Motives?   │
                  └──────┬───────┘       └──────┬─────┘
                         │                      │
                         ↓                      ↓ Robbery?
                  ┌──────────────┐
                  │ Possible     │
                  │ Outcomes     │
                  └──┬────────┬──┘
                     ↓        ↓
              ┌─────────┐  ┌────────┐
              │Freedom? │  │ Death? │
              └─────────┘  └────────┘
```

"Are we ever going to get a break?" Ivor complained.

"Patience" DS Jobb replied.

Ivor snorted.

"Patience comes to those who wait"

"She might already be dead"

"You're a cheerful soul"

"You should know that by now"

A knock on the door, interrupted them. The desk sergeant put his head, round the door.

"Sir, this just came" he said putting a parcel on the table.

"Any doughnuts?"

"How about you get out of here?"

The desk sergeant stuck his tongue out, and retreated. DS Jobb opened the parcel, and tipped it upside down.

"Sir" he said sharply.

Ivor looked up at the tone.

Arthur slid on a pair of gloves, he kept in the desk drawer, and removed the contents of the parcel.

There was a recorded DVD and a note from Eddie Rabin, the missing girl's father.

DI Gunn, DS Jobb

This arrived for me this morning. I have hidden it from my wife.

This would just upset her. However I thought you should see it.

It however proves, that until a couple of hours ago, my daughter was alive.

Edwin J. Rabin

"Play it"

Ivor gave the order. DS Jobb booted up his laptop, tapping his fingers, in a rhythm of his own devising.

"Can you stop that" Ivor snapped.

"It's distracting"

The DVD thrust into the drive, loaded and began to play.

Rose-Anna was sat on a mattress, in a room that could possibly be a cellar.

Water ran down the walls, which had turned a nasty shade of green.

Rose-Anna herself looked terrible.

Her hair stood up on end. There were black shadows under her eyes.

Not as though she had bruises, or was lacking sleep, but as though she had cried, and not been allowed to wash her face afterwards.

Her left hand was above her head, secured there by a chain in a black metal bracket.

Her right hand was loose, but there was no way she could go anywhere.

Her head was hooded. Underneath this, her mouth was taped, so she couldn't speak.

It was a sickening sight. How far had Rose-Anna's father, been able to watch this?

Ivor wanted to turn away, but he couldn't do so, in all professional conscience.

He forced himself, to continue watching.

A gloved hand, appeared in view holding a sheet of snow-white paper.

He pushed it into Rose-Anna's free hand. Automatically her muscles tensed to receive it.

The hood got taken from her head, and her mouth was suddenly nakedly free.

There was a gun barrel, to her head now. Ivor had no doubt, it was loaded.

She looked down and began to read. Her tone was expressionless.

She sounded like a robot, and looked like a vampire.

"Daddy. You have to listen to me. I haven't yet been harmed, but if you want it, to remain that way, then you've got to do everything you're told..."

"You already called the Police, but that can be overlooked, for the time being. They want £100,000 from you. You have a 72 hour deadline. Please Daddy. Get me out of here. I don't want to get hurt"

She looked up and her chocolate brown eyes, wore a haunted look that, she shouldn't have gained, for at least another 30 years.

In the last few days, those eyes had seen far too much.

Then everything went back, to how it had been at the beginning.

The screen went suddenly black. DS Jobb switched off the laptop.

He was subconsciously chewing his fingernails, biting sideways to remove the quick.

"Well?" he said.

"I think they're deadly serious" Ivor's tone was bleak.

The shrill ring of the telephone, on the desk made them jump.

Arthur lunged across the desk, to answer it. It was like a despairing goalkeeper, lunging for a football shot, he knows he will never have a chance of saving, but he is expected to try anyway, so he makes the attempt.

He caught it on the third ring. He listened and then put his hand, over the mouthpiece.

"That was the bank manager, who runs the branch where Rose-Anna works. He said a rather large sum of money, has come up in the system, and he needs to approve it, before it moves any further"

"How large?" Ivor demanded sharply.

"He says it moves into the millions, at least five"

"Ask him to authorise it. We have just less than 72 hours. Our chances of finding her, will be much better, if we don't do anything that, might cause them to decide to bring that deadline forward."

DS Jobb nodded, told the bank manager to authorise the transaction, and hung up the phone.

"Ring Rose-Anna's father, get him to come in. Then get that envelope, off to the lab, see if there's any fingerprints"

Arthur nodded, picked up the envelope, in his gloved hands and left the room.

Ivor buried his head in his hands.

Chapter Eight

Eddie Rabin tried to hide the strain, his daughter's disappearance had caused, as he sat across from Ivor and Arthur.

"I'll never ever forget that, as long as I live. My daughter needs me, and I can't help her. I don't have that kind of money, and have no prospect of ever raising it" his tone was desperate.

"I'm not sure, whether to show Heidi or not. What if it's the last time Rose..."

He couldn't continue. He fumbled in his suit jacket, and extracted his cigarettes.

Up until the last few days, he'd not smoked since he was a teen, trying to look cool.

Without comment, DS Jobb produced a foil ashtray, from the top of a filing cabinet.

Eddie was struggling to light the cigarette. His hands were shaking, far too much for the flame, coming from the lighter to stay alight.

"Should I?" Arthur enquired.

Eddie nodded and Arthur took the lighter, and unlit cigarette from his hands.

He lit it with a practised hand, and passed it back to the man, who looked tried, sentenced and condemned to death.

The death penalty, might not exist in Britain anymore, and hadn't since 1964, but it was a death sentence all the same.

It was the first time, he'd shown any real concern for Rose-Anna.

It had seemed like too much bother, parenthood until now.

He had taken it for granted, and had a feeling that he was about to learn, a sharp and extremely harsh lesson. It certainly didn't seem fair.

He smoked the cigarette, down to the end, spreading ash everywhere.

He answered the questions, as best as he could. Had the postman delivered the package? What time? Blah, blah blah.

By the time the interview was over, there were nearly a whole 10 deck, smouldering away in the ashtray.

The air seemed polluted, as it entered his lungs, on emerging from the police station.

Now, all he had to do, was tell Heidi that Rose-Anna, was more than likely doomed.

It wasn't a pleasant prospect.

Heidi was home when he arrived. Where else would she be?

She was scrubbing the bath out, with a fierceness that was unwarranted.

It was as though, the bath had committed the crime, and she was punishing it accordingly.

She looked up as he entered, bright yellow Marigold rubber gloves, up to her elbows, bleached sponge turned upwards, as though she had paused mid scrub.

"Good day?" she asked, as though on autopilot.

"Not particularly" he answered carefully.

"I um… need to talk to you, Heid," he added hesitantly.

She turned round and stared. He very rarely shortened her name these days.

"You might want to sit down"

His tone was unusually kind. His face strangely soft. His eyes were the same shade, as Rose-Anna's. She hadn't noticed this for several years.

"Ed, you're scaring me" she said.

She stripped off the gloves, and he took hold of her shoulders, and took her gently but firmly into the master bedroom.

She sank down on the bed, and waited for him to speak.

He however did not sit with her. This behaviour was creepy in itself.

"Ed?" she prompted.

He held up a hand, not sure how to start.

"I um got called into the police station this morning"

He broke off, as she let out her breath.

"I'm fine. I'm fine. Just, just, just tell me, please"

"OK, but it's not easy, you're not going to like it"

She nodded to acknowledge his warning, but did nothing else.

"I went to work this morning, and the postman delivered a parcel. It seemed strange. But I opened it anyway. There was this DVD. I watched it and..." he couldn't complete the story.

"And...?" she prompted gently, not sure whether she wanted him to continue anyway.

"It was my worst fucking nightmare. Rose is alive, as of this morning. She's OK I suppose. She was definitely abducted on Saturday. I, we have 72 hours from the viewing of the DVD, to give them the ransom money, or else she..."

Heidi didn't need him, to complete the sentence this time.

"You have got the money"

It was a statement, not a question. He shook his head.

"No I don't. I can't raise it in time either"

She said nothing, not trusting herself to speak presumably.

He hated it when she was this silent. It usually meant trouble.

He could see her eyes glistening, and turned away while she shed the tears.

He held out his arms, once she was done and after staring at him for a few seconds, almost to the point, that he withdrew them again, she melted into him.

He winced inwardly, as she ruined his best white shirt. He said nothing, just held her.

She hadn't allowed this much intimacy, since her mother had died 2 years before.

He reminded himself, that this was unimportant. A shirt was a material object, and could be replaced, his daughter couldn't.

Chapter Nine

Rose-Anna was starting to feel, extremely lonely now. She hadn't spoken to anyone in days.

She knew the deadline was ticking down. Every morning, she asked on the state of the ransom, but they said nothing.

Did that mean, it hadn't been paid, or had it and they didn't want to tell her, to make her suffer?

Well, she was certainly doing that.

There were images in her head, which she didn't want there.

She was counting her heartbeats, knowing that any one of them, could be her last.

Thud! Thud! Thud! Thud! Thud!

It was a strangely comforting sound. Her days were so boring these days.

She didn't know, whether she should be worried or not. Her life was in the hands of her father.

Would he come through in time? He was none too reliable sometimes.

He could be flaky at times and easily bored, meaning he never concentrated on any task for long. She hoped she would be pleasantly surprised.

The clock was counting down, like that fucking clock in the TV show 24, only this time Jack Bauer was not going to ride to the rescue, like her own personal knight in shining armour.

All the time, his daughter was thinking this Eddie Rabin himself, was trying his best to beg and borrow money.

People had started to put two and two together.

Those who before had looked confused, when asked about Rose-*Anna,* rather than just Rose, were now recognising both names.

He himself, had been temporarily suspended from work.

The company were presumably, putting profits before concern, for their employees.

They presumably thought, that an abducted daughter was far too distracting.

His credit rating, was a little black so the bank wouldn't give him a loan.

There were loan sharks, which were obviously illegal and dangerous.

There were no rules, governing the behaviour of loan sharks.

They were well within their rights to break bones. He shuddered at the very thought.

He hadn't got very far. He'd checked their bank balance, and found that he had less, than a quarter of the amount needed.

He tried not to think. The only thought in his head, was that his daughter, was definitely going to die, and when she did, it would be entirely his fault.

He had never felt so desperate, in his whole life.

Chapter Ten

9:00 am Deadline Day, Greater Manchester Police Headquarters

DI Ivor Gunn faced today, with some trepidation. They would all sink or swim by today. He had been working for hours, and got nowhere.

He sorted through the post. Rose-Anna's father, had left him another note.

DS Jobb had photocopied it for him.

The ink used by Eddie Rabin, had originally been blue, but the photocopier was old and photocopied, only in black and white and blotchily.

DI Gunn, DS Jobb

Midnight tonight. The warehouses. Don't have the money. Not sure what to do.
Need a plan
Edwin Rabin

This was why, he'd come up with a plan. It involved the armed response unit.

He'd rung Cameron Hammond, the leader of the pack, so to speak.

Cameron was professional, in the best and worst of circumstances.

He had somehow handled, his own uncle and aunt's murders.

But that hadn't been Ivor's case.

Cameron had got a personal revenge, taking out the man responsible, for ripping his family to pieces.

DS Steven Potter had retired, from the force in the wake of the incident.

The case had taken three years, to come to a satisfactory conclusion.

It had all started, with his best friend Darren Hunter's wife, going missing. It was an abduction case, rather like this one.

There had been times, when Steven confessed to thinking, Laurel Hunter's life was over.

However, she had been found, barely alive, but still breathing.

She had been nursed back to health, by the confident and most definitely expert attentions, of Doctor Adrian Benson.

She had been reunited with her husband, but they had never rested easy.

Ivor sincerely hoped, no one needed Doctor Benson's professional expertise tonight.

The Hunters, had practically spent the three remaining years of their lives running.

Former DS Potter had spent, the best part of seven years now, learning to live with actions, he'd taken and couldn't take back.

The Hunters had faced many more dangerous situations.

They had been paying for a crime, which was never theirs to atone for.

Darren's father Joseph Hunter; himself a Former DI of Greater Manchester Police, had during an evening of misadventure, run over and killed a young woman and her 3 year old daughter.

He had been drunk, so he had abandoned his father's car, and along with his three companions, had fled the scene.

He had sought refuge at a pub in Preston, Lancashire, which rented rooms.

His stay had been a week long, and he had charmed the landlord's daughter.

He had subsequently married her. He had fathered a child with her.

But Joseph had been a womaniser, and baby Darren, was by no means, the only child he fathered. To this day, no one knew the exact number.

He and Angie had remained married, despite much provocation, for her to divorce him, right up until the day he widowed her, some 6 years ago, 2 years before the death of their son and daughter-in-law.

But perhaps she was now, on the verge of happiness once again.

She was engaged to be married, to the man she'd been dating, when Joseph first appeared on the scene.

His name was Finn something, and though Joseph had been her soul mate, she was determined to live out the rest of her life with someone; she might not remarry though because she was 77 years old after all.

She said she owed it to Darren after all. She visited his grave whenever possible.

DI Gunn had been to the forest, where the dark deed took place.

A dark blood-spattered X, marked the spot, and Ivor would have cause to remember this, before not too much longer had passed.

Someone had deliberately scored that mark there, using both Laurel and Darren's blood.

That was according to pathologist Byron Baron anyway.

That was someone else, Ivor hoped none of them saw that evening.

It was said the forest contained, the restless spirits of all the people who'd died there, and there had been a lot.

Ellie Ryan, the famous disabled actress, had drowned in the lake there, Laurel and Darren Hunter just to name a few.

DI Gunn had a few cases of his own, which he knew he should have handled better.

The case dubbed "The Zodiac Conspiracy, several 15 year old girls had gone missing and then photographs had been taken of fresh tattoos, in the shape of a sign of the Zodiac.

Aries down to Virgo, before the madman responsible was stopped.

Then had come the Matherson girl. University students Zachary (Zach) Mayhew and Daniel (Danny) Webb, had been accused of the murder, of fellow student Chloe Matherson.

Chloe, had suffered from the condition Cerebral Palsy. The twist was that Zach was blind, and Danny was autistic.

Danny's father was Curtis Webb, the Deputy Prime Minister, and MP for Preston.

Chloe had suffocated, for some reason. Zachary and Danny had been defended, by eminent barrister Lee Saddle, but had been convicted.

After a short spell in prison, their convictions had been quashed, and they had been released.

Zach was now, a bestselling true crime author.

Curtis Webb had used the sympathy, generated from his son's mistaken imprisonment, to win his seat in Parliament again, in the recent election.

He was supporting a campaign, by blind actor Jake Marshall, himself once wrongly arrested, for the abduction of his then 5-year old, now 10-year old grandson, Jimmi-Eric Marshall.

Jake was now on his 6th or 7th marriage and had children by most of his wives.

Little Jimmi-Eric's father Kyle Marshall, was one of Jake's sons with Ellie.

For some reason, they hadn't trusted the Police, to handle the case, and Ellie had mysteriously met her death, in Madeley Forest.

Ivor strongly suspected, that Jake knew the circumstances, but he had always remained tight-lipped, about his first ex-wife's final hour.

That hadn't been Ivor's case either, but he had had the Memory Lane School one.

Student Tanya Parker, had apparently hung herself, and then fallen into the swimming pool, in 2013.

Years later, murders had started happening, in a copycat fashion, so Ivor had been given the case.

The murderer had died in prison recently; he'd been suffering from an inoperable brain tumour.

But it was his most recent case, which rankled the most with Ivor.

An expelled student, Chandler Jackson had taken a fellow student, and two teaching assistants hostage.

He was American and terrified, he was going to be extradited, back to New York to face trial.

After the terrorist attacks of 11th September 2001, the Americans tended to act first, ask questions and apologize later.

At first, Ivor had been in charge, but a few days later, when the stalemate hadn't been broken, his superiors had replaced him, with Former DS Potter, who'd been persuaded out of retirement.

The case had been resolved peacefully. All hostages were safe, and it had emerged that Chandler, was being manipulated, and the real culprit, was the Italian deputy headmaster of the school.

He was due to stand trial, at some point next year, and barrister Lee Saddle, would be prosecuting counsel.

His goose, was probably already cooked.

Ivor's superiors had told him, that Former DS Potter would be advising this evening, but that he, Ivor was in charge.

He intended to keep it that way.

They would have a meeting, before the kick-off and Former DS Potter, would be there, along with everyone else.

Chapter Eleven

9:30pm Deadline Day

Rose-Anna Rabin was shivering. She was well aware, that it was fright.

She knew what day it was. They hadn't let her forget. Her guards, had been taunting her all day.

She now felt like a turkey at Christmas. They had combed her hair, which had felt like a violation.

It had been dyed tomato red, rather than its usual brown.

It had grown in length, and it was now long enough to be plaited.

She had done this herself. The amount of knots in her hair, had made her want to scream.

It hadn't been brushed since that Saturday.

They had allowed her to shower, but with ice-cold water.

She didn't mind particularly, it was just good, to not be able to smell the sweetness of her own body odour, and dirt.

She had been given fresh clothes, which she had at least, been allowed to change herself.

She now wore, a white blouse, which she would never have chosen herself.

A black pleated skirt, far too short to be worn in winter, had replaced the trousers. A leather jacket, which was not her own, was over it.

Her shoes were slightly tight, possibly too small. She would have blisters if she ever got the chance, to take them off again.

They were high-heeled, and she didn't wear them very often.

Her hands were in a familiar position, secured behind her back by handcuffs.

They were on the highest, tightest notch and were painful, not to mention cold.

If she twisted her wrist, it would break.

But she knew, there was no point in complaining.

They wouldn't have done anything about it, just laughed or worst still, hit her round the head.

The leather jacket, hid the handcuffs from sight.

Her legs were tied securely with rope. The friction was burning her.

They would have to carry her, when the time came.

She stared at the hood, which would later go over her head.

For now though, it lay harmlessly in the corner, waiting patiently to resume duty.

She had developed a severe hatred for the thing.

She could taste the silver tape, stretched over her mouth.

She was surprised, they'd let her breathe at all. Her tongue was just touching it.

It tasted of glue. They had used nearly an entire roll. She was now just waiting, for fate to play out.

Someone consulted a watch.

"Time to go"

"Duck" his companion said.

She bowed her head. They had worn the fight, out of her a long time ago.

She had given up, become dependent and institutionalised.

She ate, spoke and shit on command. But her eyes followed him, as he crossed the room.

He snatched up the hood. She sighed as it rolled back over her head.

It was starting to smell musty. She was however, resigned.

She tried to stand up, but stood no chance. She had to sit back down hard, on her bottom again.

There was a loud sound, possibly exasperation.

The floor vibrated, as someone walked across it. She counted the seconds, before she felt herself being tipped upside down.

It is very uncomfortable, to be carried over someone's shoulder like luggage. You bounce around with every step.

The small whimpering sounds, she couldn't help making, were stifled in the wad of tape. She could feel the blood rushing to her head.

She shook her head, as she was set the right way up. She must have been put in the van. because she could hear the doors slamming.

Her thoughts were running, at 100 miles an hour. Would she survive the night or not?

These were quite possibly her final hours on Earth.

She jumped as the engine roared, and the van began to move.

She overbalanced as it did so. She cursed under her breath, as her elbow bashed on the floor.

She tried to remember, what direction they were going in, but gave up pretty quickly.

She found herself, counting in her head once again.

After what felt like hours, the van stopped. She was back over the thug's shoulder, once more.

It was freezing wherever they were. It was the middle of winter, and had apparently begun to snow earlier. The leather jacket, seemed thin protection against the elements.

The thug set her down, on her feet again. She staggered, but the man's grip on her, kept her upright.

He dragged her backwards, presumably into the shadows. Now all they had to do, was wait.

Chapter Twelve

9:30pm Greater Manchester Police Headquarters

The planning meeting, was now in progress. Ideas were discussed and rejected.

"We have the suitcase, with the right amount of money, but they'll be expecting Rose-Anna's father"

"We can't let him go in alone. We have to protect him"

"No. Not if that's how they want it. I won't put my daughter, at any unnecessary risk" Eddie Rabin's voice was firm and sharp.

"Sir, you can't ask us to do that"

"I can. Rose is my daughter"

Cameron must have been born, with the same diplomatic genes, as his uncle.

"Let's talk about it later. The main priority is Rose-Anna and her safety. I've been on operations, when things go south and it isn't good"

"It's going to be easy" someone said.

It was a young, inexperienced member of Cameron's team.

"Shut up Appleby" Tom Stone said.

"Could you shoot a bullet, when someone is holding a hostage, and using them as a shield?" Cameron asked.

"Yeah. We do it all the time in training"

"Training is different" Cameron muttered.

"How is it?"

"Because if you get it wrong, someone dies" Tom Stone snapped.

"In training, you get to try again, with the next *paper* target. Human beings aren't made of paper, David"

The youngster always got on Tom's nerves. He was far too cocky, for his own good.

"I've half a mind, to send you home" Cameron said.

"No don't. We all need to learn sometime" Tom said, winking in Cameron's direction.

"Who was it said, a sharp blow to the head, is much better than living in ignorance your whole life?"

"My uncle, just before he'd box with my dad" Cameron replied with a grin.

"And who won?" Tom asked.

"My uncle mostly"

"Because?"

"He knew when to dodge. He had the experience, to know when to give up, and when to fight. So did my aunt"

"Precisely, if they didn't fight, it wasn't because what they were doing wasn't worth it, but because fighting isn't always how you win. You just have to pick your moments"

"Right. Now that's established. I'll be outside" Cameron said.

DS Steven Potter followed him. Cameron was standing, leaning against the wall.

"Are you OK?" he asked.

"Yeah. Talking about them. It..."

"I know.

"Will we ever get over it? Dad is like a 6 year old. He might as well, put his fingers in his ears, and hum loudly every time they get mentioned"

"Your Aunt Bella is the same"

"You saw her recently. How is she?"

"Coping. Kind of"

"I commune with them, before every job. It helps me remember, that life isn't permanent" Cameron said.

He bowed his head.

His eyes didn't leave the ground, for several seconds, perhaps minutes.

Finally he sighed deeply, and looked up.

Steven was half-convinced, he would get down on his knees and pray, but he didn't.

Cameron's faith was as lapsed, as Rueben's and Darren's was.

He might have been Christened Catholic, but partly due to his mother, who was part of the Church of England.

She was no more religious, than Rueben was.

The faith was just a symbol. None of the Hammond children, had been inside a church, more than a handful of times.

"OK then. Let's get this show on the road" Cameron said finally.

Chapter Thirteen

Midnight, Warehouse, Undisclosed location

It was very much the stuff of nightmares. The moon beamed down, watching proceedings.

Owls hooted in trees and animals rustled.

The date should have been Halloween. It would have seemed appropriate.

There would be plenty of ghosts, disturbed that evening.

Cameron Hammond directed his men, to all the best vantage points.

The warehouse was still dark, so they were unsure, whether they were there or not.

DI Ivor Gunn, DS Jobb and Former DS Steven Potter, stood with Eddie Rabin.

There was sweat, breaking out on the man's forehead. He periodically wiped it away, with his sleeve.

He was also shaking slightly.

He would like to pretend with cold. It was after all cold enough, to have snow in the air.

His daughter took after him, in the sense that she couldn't stand, to show any kind of weakness to anyone.

His breath came out in quick, sharp gusts of steam, visible in the frosty air,

Ivor was not at all convinced, Eddie could handle this, but he was not about to voice this opinion.

It would just be extremely counterproductive.

They had no choice, but to do things this way, if they wanted even a remote chance, of getting Rose-Anna back safely.

"Ready?" Ivor asked her father.

He nodded.

Steven pushed a briefcase full of money, Eddie's way. Eddie grasped it, like he would a lifebelt, should he be in a swimming pool, and be drowning.

He looked at his watch, and gulped nervously, as the hand ticked past the hour mark.

He began walking, as though he was going to the guillotine.

The padlock was unlocked, and it was pitch black inside.

He stood waiting for something to happen.

A sudden light blinded him. He threw up his hand, to shield his eyes.

He stumbled slightly, into some stacked palettes. They clattered to the floor, making him jump.

The palettes would have been familiar, to Laurel and Darren Hunter.

The Timberlake family's property, had been auctioned off, but it was still being put, to much the same use.

Eddie cursed. The cold metal of a gun barrel, against his spine made him freeze.

"Put the briefcase down on the floor, and turn to the wall"

Eddie did as he was told.

The search was methodical, for hidden wires he presumed.
They were evidently satisfied however.

"Where's my daughter?" he asked.

"She's here. She's fine"

"I want to see her"

"All in good time"

"The deal was, I pay the ransom and I get my daughter back alive. How do I know, she's still alive if I don't see her?"

"Fair point" the thug said reasonably.

He clicked his fingers sharply. Another thug came into view.

He threw Rose-Anna down, so she skidded across the floor, a few metres on her knees.

She grunted involuntarily, as she hit the floor.

"Satisfied?" the thug asked.

"No not really" Eddie replied.

The man he was "negotiating" with, sighed and nodded. He was suddenly staring into his own eyes. The look in them was pleading.

She probably would have spoken to him, had she been able to.

The sight of his daughter, in the state she was, made him want to be sick.

"Rose? You OK? Been treated properly sweetheart"

He watched as Rose nodded twice, once in answer to each question, she'd been asked.

She reminded him briefly, of the nodding dog Churchill, in the insurance adverts.

The man in charge motioned, but again Rose-Anna's father intervened.

"Don't put that thing back over her head. If you're going to kill her, it's kind of cowardly, to do it when she can't see it coming. You guys aren't cowards"

He said the words, but they didn't compute with his thoughts.

The leader scowled, but didn't give the order again.

Instead the barrel of the gun, pressed against Rose-Anna's head. He had no doubt, it was loaded.

It was close enough that, if he was to pull the trigger, there was no way the bullet, would miss going straight to her cerebral cortex.

She would die instantly. Painlessly maybe but dead all the same.

Eddie nudged the briefcase towards the man, who bent and gathered it up.

Eddie shivered at the thought, of anything penetrating his daughter's cerebral cortex.

"It's all there. May I take my daughter home now?" he asked.

"It needs to be counted"

Eddie nodded his understanding. He'd been expecting this.

"You can't take my word for it, in case I have short-changed you, taken my daughter back, and then you'd have nothing" he said.

"5:00 in the morning, Madeley Forest. Be there" was the parting shot.

The tone it was uttered in, was like chilled steel. It sent shivers down Eddie's spine.

It was not a command, he dared disobey.

Chapter Fourteen

Heidi Rabin rolled over on the sofa. She'd been pretending to sleep on it, as her husband walked back through the door of their home.

She switched the TV over. She had been watching the 24 hour news, praying to God that there wouldn't be reports of a female body found murdered.

Or a male one, if they had killed Rose, there was no guarantee, they'd leave Eddie alive to tell the tale.

There hadn't been but she was not comforted. She would relax only, when Rose was safe and back in her sight.

She would ground the girl, and forbid her to go out ever again, if she had to.

She didn't call out to him, but waited with mounting impatience, for him to make an appearance.

This he did. five minutes or so later. He went straight to the drinks cabinet, and poured himself a whiskey, drinking it down in one.

Was this a good sign or a bad one? She couldn't decide. She would know, if he met her eyes, and from the first word he spoke.

He sat down in his regular armchair. She waited for him to face her.

An uneasy silence stretched between them. Finally she could stand it no longer.

"So?" she said.

He turned towards her.

"I saw Rose" he replied.

"Is she...?"

"She's alive for now"

"For now?" her tone was sharp.

"I gave them the money. They need to count it. I'm supposed to go back at 5:00"

"I'm coming with you" she said.

"Oh no you're not"

"Edwin!"

"No Heidi. You haven't seen her. She's not Rose anymore. I've never seen her that frightened. She's pretending not to be, typical Rose. You don't want to see her like that. God knows what they've done, but she's broken, in spirit at least."

"What have they done to my daughter?"

"Last time I checked, Rose-Anna was *our* daughter"

His tone was icier, than he meant it to be. He sighed.

"I need to make sure she's safe. I can't do that, if you come along too. It's dangerous Heidi"

"I can't just sit here, and wait hours to know if I still have two daughters or one"

"I'll let you know, as soon as I can"

"Promise?"

"I promise with cherries on top" he promised.

They sat in silence, for the remaining time he was in the house.

Chapter Fifteen

3am Timberlake Towers, the basement cellar

Rose-Anna Rabin sat in her cell. It had almost become home now.

She was sat on the mattress, which had become her own personal sanctuary.

She was chained to the wall once again, both hands this time.

The silver tape, was still in place over her mouth. The hood mercifully, had been left off her head.

It had been strange, seeing her father this evening. He had seemed like an entirely different person.

The situation though, was still unclear. She still wasn't sure, she would survive the night.

She was once again, counting her heartbeats. She enjoyed hearing them.

They meant she was still alive, for now at least.

The thugs had left her alone, since bringing her back here. Presumably they were counting their fortune.

Gabrielle Cullen looked up, as the sacks were put on the desk, in front of her.

Slowly they were tipped upside down, so that the notes flopped, and the coins rattled round in circles.

She started sorting them into piles. The notes got bundled together by someone. There must be at least 1000 there.

She was planning ahead for later. She was expecting a challenge to her authority.

Wayne had gone back to his home. She would not have him hurt, for all the gold in the world.

He was innocent of everything. Getting him injured, would achieve nothing.

He and his wife, had patched up their differences and he'd departed earlier in the day.

He'd text her to say, he was safely home where he should be.

The counting of the money, was done by 4:00. Wait for it. Wait for it, a small voice in her brain said.

Almost on cue, the lead thug drew his gun. She smiled. It was a smile, which could freeze steel.

"Planning a coup?" she asked pleasantly.

"Shut up bitch"

"Do you think I haven't been expecting this?"

"I said shut up"

"Or you'll do what?"

"You'll die"

"Do you think I want to live, like this for a second longer, if I don't have to? This body is useless. OK I'm luckier than most, I'll acknowledge that. But it will never be enough, to consider myself lucky, to count my blessings and to rely on the healing hands of God. Miracle worker he might be, but he's busy"

She paused as though for thought.

"Duh, metal brain; you'd be doing me a favour. I get to be with my angel, and see his hazel eyes and black curls again. Eyes so like his daddy's. I'll get to be in my husband's arms again, and tell him I don't blame him at all, for the decision he made."

Only a few words of this speech, seemed to have penetrated the gunman's skull.

"What did you call me?"

"Metal brain, Thick"

She had goaded him enough. She saw his finger, curl round the trigger.

The report of the bullet, was extremely loud in the room.

She saw it flying towards her. She could have ducked, but she didn't bother.

The bullet hit her, squarely in the chest. Her heart got out one more beat.

He had done exactly, what she wanted and martyred her.

Her murderer walked casually over, and felt for a pulse. There wasn't one. He hadn't really expected to feel one.

None too gently, he pulled the corpse out of the wheelchair. He would have to dispose of it, at some point.

A pain in the ass, but necessary if he wanted to escape undetected.

He had plans for this money and no one, not Gabrielle Cullen, not Rose-Anna Rabin was going to get in his way.

He could get out of this game for good. Retire to his country cottage in Wales.

He left the room, and went down to the basement cellar. He saw the terrified young woman, looking up at him.

He had a daughter, about the same age as her, but it didn't soften him.

"Just so you know. There's been a change of leadership. I'm not going to be nearly so kind to you, as Gabrielle was" he snarled.

Rose-Anna's face visibly paled.

She was presumably remembering how "kind" Gabrielle had been to her.

It had included, the near amputation of a finger, and an eyeball after all.

She was obviously wondering, if they were still on the cards.

"You do as you're told. Understand?"

Rose-Anna didn't answer. Had she been able to, she wouldn't have, because her mouth was dry.

Spit clung to the roof of her mouth.

"I said do you understand" the thug repeated.

He produced a knife from his pocket. Rose-Anna nodded quickly.

She didn't know what else to do. She didn't want him, to decide that she wasn't going to answer.

He might decide to carve her up, to a new design of his own devising.

She didn't want him, to carve a star on her stomach or anything like that.

She could just imagine, how painful that would be.

"Good!" was all he said.

The word came out as a snarl, so threatening she jumped nearly a foot in the air.

She groaned, as the handcuffs dug into her wrists.

She was sure, if you looked under the handcuffs, you'd probably have seen, a trickle of crimson blood.

Chapter Sixteen

Madeley Forest 5:00am

Appropriately, the moon shone down, casting shadows, looking like spilled silver paint.

The trees rustled peacefully, but up in his tree, Cameron Hammond could see, the dark patch cut in the forest floor.

The X scored in his aunt and uncle's blood, gave him the creeps, seen in this profile anyway.

He checked the rifle's sight, a final time. He tested the action.

It was unhampered. He had remembered the phrase "Take care of your equipment, and your equipment will take care of you"

He would be in radio contact, with his team at all times. He was wearing what felt like, several tonnes of body armour.

The Police team on the ground, were getting edgy. The opposing force was late.

DI Gunn wasn't sure, what this meant and therefore everyone was nervous.

But they didn't want, to make the first move. Nobody was as yet sure, of the fate of Rose-Anna Rabin, and to that end, they had to tread carefully.

Eddie Rabin checked his watch. His eyes like everyone else's drawn to the X.

Former DS Steven Potter stood next to him. He was quivering, it wasn't fear it was rage. His lips moved in a silent vibration.

There had been many debates, over the centuries on the power of prayer, and Eddie was unsure where he stood on the God question. His wife was deeply atheist.

This was the reason, they had married in the local Registry Office.

Neither Elizabeth-Ellen nor Rose-Anna, had been christened.

Perhaps this would become relevant, this evening. It was said by religious people, that you didn't ascend to Heaven, when you died if you weren't Christened, but spent Eternity in Purgatory.

Had they done the wrong thing, for Rose-Anna by not christening her?

Would God look down his nose at her, once she was in the queue to enter Heaven?

Perhaps it wasn't too late, to remedy that situation? Was this argument with himself pointless? Almost certainly.

A loud roaring sound, announced the arrival of the main players.

Nobody moved, as the van parked in the trees. The sound of thuds. The doors closing?

Then a man came into sight. He was carrying something heavy, over his shoulder. He wasn't even sweating.

There was a grunt, as the bundle was put down on the ground.

He set it upright. It was Rose-Anna then. Eddie felt sick. Whatever they were going to do, they should do it quickly.

He stepped forward, into the light of the moon.

"Does my daughter get to walk free?" he asked.

The thug considered him.

"We had a deal. A gentleman doesn't go back on his word" Eddie continued.

"It wasn't my word. But a gentleman doesn't go back on a lady's word either" the thug replied.

"Particularly when she is not here, to honour it herself"

Eddie dearly wanted to ask, why the "lady" in question wasn't here to honour her word, but didn't dare.

He thought he knew anyway.

"However, a deal is a deal"

He took the hood from Rose-Anna's head, and the tape from her mouth.

He bent to undo the handcuffs. Rose swayed slightly. Her chocolate eyes looked unfocused. Eddie was sure she was drugged.

In fact she was. She'd been given it, when she'd finally been given a bottle of water to drink.

The new boss had held it for her. He'd given it to her, not because he intended to do anything to her, but because he wasn't entirely monstrous.

He had been told before, that if you had to kill someone, it should be done painlessly.

A bullet to the brain was quick, but if she was drugged, Rose-Anna would be too stoned, to feel anything anyway.

Perhaps he really did, intend to free her and keep his word.

Honour amongst thieves, but no one would ever know. Fate is decided on the smallest things.

David Appleby the young recruit, moved where he sat in his tree. Perhaps he was trying to re-position his gun, maybe his foot slipped, they would never know.

The master criminal's head whipped round.

"What was that?"

"What was what?" Eddie asked innocently.

"That sound?"

"Maybe an animal. It is a forest after all" Eddie suggested helpfully.

He was so close, to securing his daughter's freedom. All he had to do was think.

He could find a way out of this. He was an intelligent man after all.

"Did you bring anyone with you?"

"No. That wasn't part of the deal"

The man was like a human polygraph. He read the lie immediately.

"No it wasn't" he agreed calmly.

Then the whole world, seemed to explode like a box of fireworks, on Bonfire Night.

Chapter Seventeen

What came next was very confused. No one who survived it, could give an accurate account.

Rose-Anna had sensed the danger, and tried to get away from him, but she was still hampered by her restraints, and her head, felt like it had cotton wool, stuffed inside it.

There was an annoying buzzing sound in her ears, like an angry bee was stuck there.

As a result of both of these things, she hadn't got very far.

The thug reached out an almost casual hand, and jerked her back by the leather jacket she still wore. He reached into his back pocket.

The pistol appeared there, as if by magic and everyone's eyes followed it.

It was hypnotic. Time seemed to slow, stop and then start once more, in slow motion.

The gunman's nerve almost quailed; he might have been developing a conscience.

But then his nerve, hardened to steel again.

He didn't want to do this, he would take no pleasure in the act, but a broken deal was a broken deal. There were consequences, and her father had to learn this. He was going to lose his daughter after all.

Rose-Anna herself froze. She could feel the brush of the barrel, against the side of her head.

It was gentle almost like a lover's caressing hands. She knew she was entering, the final few seconds of her life.

There was no escaping it. She had known from the minute, she had left the garage in the hands of these barbaric animals, on that fateful Saturday morning.

There had been small reprieves, along the way, moments of peace, glimmers of hope, but they would amount to nothing.

She had always known this.

Somehow once again, her father had screwed up, let her down as he always did.

So, at just 23 years old, Rose-Anna Rabin was going to pay the ultimate price for his mistake, whatever that had been.

Gabrielle had started this. How could it have been Gabrielle?

Rose-Anna felt so betrayed. But Gabrielle was complicated. There had been a trauma in Gabrielle's life.

Rose didn't know the details. The small reference Gabrielle had made, on that Monday was it Sunday or Monday, anyway it didn't matter.

It was the only time, Gabrielle had referred to it in Rose's presence, other than to originally say, she had had a family once.

Now it seemed, that Gabrielle was dead. Rose could not hold a grudge against Gabby.

She had been in a lot of pain, both physically and emotionally.

She hoped that she was at peace now, and had found her family, as she had always wished.

Now it was her own turn, to face death Rose hoped it would be painless.

Would she get to heaven? Would there be pearly gates? Angels sat on fluffy clouds, playing harps, as she'd always imagined as a child?

Well, she would have the answer soon.

She'd have the answer to life, the answer to the universe, to everything even and she doubted that it really, would turn out to be 42.

This had been stated, in The Hitchhiker's Guide to the Galaxy, the science fiction series, created by the dead English writer and dramatist, Douglas Adams.

The tears, which unwillingly left her eyes, froze on her cheeks, as they met the frozen air of the night.

She felt his finger tighten, on the trigger and braced herself.

She thought perhaps, she should close her eyes, but it seemed like too much effort.

Besides, she didn't wish for her final vision, in this world to be nothing but black.

She heard the rush of air, and felt the impact as it slammed into her.

Then her mind was blissfully blank, and abruptly everything ended for her. Rose-Anna Rabin, ceased to exist.

As his daughter swayed, and began to fall the horrified man broke out of his trance, and ran forward.

She couldn't hit the ground, she just couldn't. That was too final.

The forest paused, as though in shock and horror, that once again, it could be the scene of a death, a killing ground.

But in reality, it was the calm before the storm. The murderer ignored Eddie Rabin completely, obviously deciding that a man, who would shortly be grieving for his daughter, would not pause to be a threat to him.

He turned his gun barrel on the trees, and pulled the trigger.

David Appleby yelped and fell out of the tree, whether he was dead or not, would have to be determined later.

Cameron Hammond was now at the base of his tree. Steven Potter turned and stared in horror, as he watched his sister's nephew face down a desperate gunman. He was paralysed by shock.

He had inherited his uncle's courage that was clear. Steven had seconds to make a decision.

He could intervene, risking widowing Kayla, leaving Arthur, Merlin, Lance and Gwynn fatherless.

Or he could allow the maniac, to end Cameron's life. His sister would be grieving again, so would Rueben.

Another of the Hunter bloodline, would be gone. One of Darren's complicated bloodline.

He had hesitated to act before, with fatal consequences. Could he stand by, and allow history to repeat itself?

The kids or Cameron? The kids or Cameron? The kids or Cameron?

He saw Belladonna's face, tear streaked crying over Cameron's body, mascara running down her cheeks. She was cursing him.

The image faded and reformed itself. Belladonna crying again, but this time the body was his.

She half-turned her head.

The expression on her face, made up his mind for him. He threw himself across the ground, in a spectacular dive.

The gunman was distracted, giving Cameron time to run around him.

The gunman was not slow. His gun was at Steven's head, faster than you could say "bullet."

Cameron watched in horror. Steven was as calm as anything.

"Go on then. Do it. I'm ready to pay for my sins" Steven told the gunman.

How could Steven be so ready to die?

Cameron knew the answer.

He thought that Uncle Darren's and Aunt Laurel's deaths, had been his fault, because he had not handled things properly during the original investigation.

He thought that by dying, he would feel less guilty and have paid back, some of the terrible debt, he felt he owed them.

But this would be the last thing, Uncle Darren wanted, because Steven was Aunt Bella's brother too.

Uncle Darren would know, that Aunt Bella had suffered much pain, on Darren's own account, and would want to spare her anymore.

Uncle Darren would be mad, that they had felt so much pain, on his behalf.

Steven had spared Cameron presumably, from the same desire.

Aunt Bella and Dad would be heartbroken, if he Cameron died, and they would never have a chance of healing.

Cameron searched around him, but he had dropped his weapon, at the base of the tree.

He cursed. He suddenly seized upon a tree branch, lying on the ground.

He couldn't allow Steven to martyr himself, on the very ground where Uncle Darren and Aunt Laurel, had been executed.

At least not for the reasons, he appeared to want to be.

Cameron ran forward, and slugged the gunman with the branch, the gunman grunted, and Steven seeming to come to his senses, dropped to the ground.

The gun discharged and Steven yelped, his arm a bloody mess, where the bullet had gone through, half a second before.

He was injured and in pain, but the wound wasn't fatal and permanent, as a bullet to the brain would be.

The gunman, had been unsteadied by the blow, but not knocked out.

He rolled and came to his feet. Cameron half-turned to run, but a loud bang and a searing pain in his side, brought him up short.

He dropped like a stone.

Steven screamed. "No!"

"For fuck sake stop this!"

The final shot of a bloodbath rang out, as second in command, Tom Stone took charge.

He had been awaiting, some kind of order.

He was supposed to take his orders, from DI Gunn, but Ivor seemed incapable of moving from shock, so Tom had watched with mounting horror, as first the hostage was killed, then Appleby had fallen from his tree.

The boy was dead; there was no doubt about that. If the shot hadn't got him, then the fall had broken his neck. Tom could see this, from his position.

Tom had considered pulling the trigger, when the gunman had been threatening Cameron, but Steven Potter had intervened spectacularly.

Cameron had done the same for Steven.

When Cameron had gone down the second time, Tom had officially been in charge, of the Armed Response Unit, and had made the decision, to follow Steven's command.

So he had ended it. The gunman lay spread-eagled on the ground; his gun lay in his right hand.

Chapter Eighteen

Doctor Adrian Benson stared at the scene, in front of him.

He was standing with the pathologist Byron Baron, and Doctor Thomas Seabrook.

Since Laurel and Darren's deaths, Steven Potter had taken precautions.

He always had medical support, on standby at least. Tom Stone jumped down, out of the tree he was in.

He went over to Cameron.

Cameron's breathing was laboured. He signalled to the doctors.

"You take Steve, I'll get Cameron" Adrian said to Thomas, who nodded.

"Oh by the way, is Courtney on duty tonight?" Adrian asked conversationally.

"Of course she is. Sod's law. Her parents and now her cousin" Thomas sighed.

"Cameron's going nowhere, if I can help it" Adrian said grimly.

Byron followed Adrian.

He went over to Rose-Anna. Her father had reached her, in time to stop her hitting the floor.

As Byron watched, he brushed a lock of hair out of her eyes.

There was blood in it, but he stroked it anyway. He closed her eyes, over her glassy stare.

"May I?" Byron asked gently.

Rose-Anna's father clutched her to him. He had wiped the tears, from his daughter's cheeks.

"You're going to put her in a bag" he said.

His tone was somewhat wild, but that was nothing compared to his eyes.

Byron knew, he would have to do this carefully.

"Your daughter's name is Rose-Anna right?"

Always use the present tense, not the past tense.

"Rose" the reply was firm.

"She hated being called Rose-Anna"

"Oh I'm sorry. It gives her full name, on my paperwork. I'll be gentle, I promise. I just need to see Rose. She'll be more comfortable"

"If I let you examine her, you'll take good care of her? She's my little girl"

"Of course. I promise" Byron said.

"I'm sorry. I know there's nothing anyone can do for her now, and it's your job. I just don't want her, to be alone. She might get lonely"

Byron was used to this. A lot of people expressed this sentiment. It might seem stupid, but Byron understood.

"She won't be on her own or lonely" he reassured him.

Eddie Rabin nodded, and began to move his daughter's head, off his lap.

Byron moved slowly, and took hold of her.

Rose-Anna's head, hadn't touched the ground, since her death.

It was as though to dirty her in any way, would be an insult, of some kind.

Eddie walked away, back firmly turned to Byron, and the work, he was doing on his daughter.

Steven Potter was agitated. Doctor Thomas Seabrook, was fighting a losing battle, and he knew it.

"Will you stay still?"

His New York accent, was still audible, even after 6 years in the UK.

"Cameron! Sort Cameron out I'm fine!"

"Adrian's sorting him out, and you certainly are not fine"

"I'll live. Just check on him. Bella and Courtney will never forgive me. Rueben will hit me, and as for Danielle..."

"You can check yourself, if you let me stop you dying, of blood loss" Thomas was exasperated.

Finally, Steven submitted to the need, for Thomas's attentions.

"The bullet needs to come out of the wound but I'm not doing it here. It's nowhere near sterile. You'd die of the infection or something, just to spite me" Thomas said.

Instead he bandaged it for now, saying he would dig it out later, as it might require an operation anyway.

This pronouncement disturbed Steven, only slightly.

Cameron groaned, but didn't open his eyes, as Adrian Benson reached him.

At least he was alive. While there was life, there was hope.

"Tom. How is he? Let me get in there"

"Not good. He's not talking" Tom Stone replied.

Adrian looked Tom over. He didn't seem to have been hurt.

He was probably, just suffering from shock. He had just seen two people die, killed one and several people had been injured.

His life would never be the same again. He might have fired, with the intention of killing before, but it was the first time, his bullet had actually taken a life.

It was Cameron's bullet, which was proven to have taken the life of Tristan Timberlake, the murderer of Darren and Laurel in the end.

"Cam, stay with me. It'll be OK. I'll sort you out. Where does it hurt?" Adrian asked.

"My side. I think I got shot. Ade, World War III will break out. Mum will go ballistic. She won't tell Dad. Let Gran know. I want my Dad"

Adrian began cutting Cameron's clothes, and probing. Cameron screamed at his touch. It was a feral sound.

"Don't worry about that. You're bleeding like a son of a bitch. It seems to have entered, through your thigh, hit the femoral artery, travelled and ended up in the abdominal cavity"

"Stop speaking Greek doc, I can't understand medical shit, and tell me what you need to do"

"Sedate you"

"What like an induced coma, like you did for Aunt Laurel and Uncle Darren a few times?"

"Yeah. You'll need to go to theatre anyway"

"Can you get on with it Doc? I don't want to be conscious, when Mum finds out, what a state I'm in" Cameron chuckled weakly and groaned again.

Chapter Nineteen

Rueben Hammond woke abruptly from sleep. His mobile phone was ringing, persistently.

He glanced blearily at the clock.

7:00 am. Who would be ringing him at this time? He checked the display.

"Adrian" flashed up on the screen.

With a feeling of unease, Rueben fumbled for it, and dropped it. He thought Adrian might ring off, but he didn't.

He finally managed to palm the phone, locate the answer button, and get his tired muscles to obey the command to push it.

"Rueben Hammond"

"Rube, its Adrian"

"Adrian this is pretty early. Shouldn't you still be on shift?"

"I'm pulling a double; perhaps triple, depending on certain factors"

"How can I help you then?"

"Rube you should sit down"

"What?"

"You should sit down. Are you on your own?"

"Yeah why?"

"Listen, I'm about to take Cameron into theatre..."

"Cameron? Our Cameron? My son Cameron?"

Rueben felt like his heart was stopping. There seemed to be something, like water in his ears.

He didn't want that question answered, that confirmation.

He groped for the edge of the bed, and sank onto it, before he fell over.

He fought to control his panic, and tuned back in.

"He seems to be bleeding internally. I couldn't keep him conscious. The bullet has entered his abdomen. From what I saw, it hit him in the thigh, and moved as he fell. It's quite a mess. I'll try my best, but..."

The fact he didn't complete the sentence, told Rueben all he needed to know.

His heart wanted to leap out of his chest. His mouth had gone dry. He swallowed.

There seemed to be a lump, in his throat.

"Does Dani...?"

"Yes"

"Thanks Ade"

"I'll keep you as informed as I can"

The world began to blur. Rueben wasn't at all sure, how he ended up dressed.

This was his worst nightmare. It was every parent's worst nightmare.

But what really hurt, were Danielle and her attitude. She had known before him, and she hadn't informed him.

Divorced they might be, but the welfare of the children, was still his business. He had thought she might remember this.

He looked up suddenly. The hairs on the back of his neck stood up.

He hadn't realized, he was being watched. But then he breathed easier.

Angela Hunter stood in the doorway. She was staying with him, for a week or two.

She had some appointment or other. He couldn't remember quite what, at the moment.

"Rueben?" she said.

Her tone was quite gentle, perhaps his face was white. Perhaps it was, that his legs were shaking, like unset jelly, even sat as he was.

"I..."

He wasn't sure how to begin. Angie ventured further into the room.

She noticed he was shaking, and took his hands in hers. She squeezed hard, and it gave him courage.

"Cameron was on duty last night. Something went wrong. I'm not sure what. He was hurt quite badly. Adrian said he was about to operate on him. He warned me, that it's touch and go. Danielle knew and she didn't tell me. I'm his father, Ang, whether she likes it or not. Does she hate me so much, that she'd only tell me, after one of my kids dies?"

His eyes sparkled, and he turned away from her, to try and hide from her, the unshed tears.

However, she wasn't fooled at all. She had seen too many shows, of male toughness for that.

Angie held out her arms, to receive him and he went into them.

She patted his head, like he wished his mother would do.

"She doesn't hate you at all. You'll find she found out and panicked. She probably wanted to get to him, as soon as possible. It's a mother's instinct. My child is hurt. If only I can get there, it'll all be better. She will have temporarily forgotten about you is all. She'll need you. She just needs to realize and remember it" Angie said reasonably.

Rueben considered this point of view. If anyone knew, how a parent felt, in a situation like this it was Angie.

The amount of times, Darren had been fighting for his very right to life.

The amount of times, she had been prepared for the worst, only to find it hadn't happened.

Except that one time when, but no he wouldn't go there not this morning.

It didn't change the fact, that Angie knew the agony of the waiting game, the unknown.

She had faced every parent's worst nightmare, countless times and had survived the experience.

She had loved and lost. She had been on the edge, and pulled herself back.

She had outlived her child, accepted and coped with that fact.

He could do worse, than take inspiration from Angela Jane Hunter.

"I need to go" Rueben said.

"You're not driving yourself" Angie snapped.

"You can't drive a Ferrari" Rueben protested.

"I bloody can. It can't be that different, from a Ford Escort" she said with a small laugh.

"You're in no state to drive" she added.

Rueben saw the wisdom of her words, nodded and walked dreamlike, to the bedside table.

He opened the drawer, and took out his car keys. He dropped them into her waiting palm.

"Good boy" she said, in the tone of a mother, speaking to a 3½ year old.

Rueben's answering grin, was watery and weak.

Chapter Twenty

Eddie Rabin stood in the pathologist's office, staring at his daughter's body.

He had been asked here, to do the formal identification.

He had been prompt at 9:00 as requested.

He had not slept at all that night. He was convinced he would never sleep again.

His wife's reaction would haunt him, until his dying day, he was sure.

He had got home, just after 6:30am. Heidi had nearly been beside herself, with agitation.

He could have sworn, there was a worn patch, where she had paced the carpet.

She had had a hopeful expression on her face, but the absence of her youngest daughter, and one look at her husband's face, had revealed the truth to her.

Her husband reminded her of a vampire. His face was ghostly pale. His eyes were bloodshot. There were shadows under his eyes.

His cheeks were dirt streaked, and it was obvious he'd been crying.

There was only one reason, he could possibly have cried. A persistent whine started in her head.

"Rose!" she practically screamed.

The denial that left her lips, was automatic and definitely inhuman.

"There was nothing I could do. It was quick and over, before she could suffer"

"How do you know she didn't suffer?" Heidi asked bleakly.

The question was not a question, but a dare. She was daring him to answer.

So he didn't answer her. There was no answer he could possibly give, to that question. She turned away from him.

She wasn't alone now. Elizabeth-Ellen was with her. Lizzie had cried, but he thought they might have been crocodile tears.

He had come here, and he reflected that you didn't know, what you had until it was gone.

His daughter was chilling in a refrigerated drawer, and he hadn't told her, half the things he'd ever wanted to. He had never been able to express, his feelings properly.

He wished he had told her, just how proud of her he was, and it was too late.

He hoped she had known somewhere deep down, without being told.

Chapter Twenty One

Marina Hemmingway was on her break. Everyone told her, she was mad still working, at 82 years old, but she just couldn't imagine retiring.

It wasn't in her nature.

One of the kids was swearing, at the computer in the teaching assistants' room.

The SENCO let certain children, do activities in the room most break times.

"You can't go in there!" Marina heard the secretary say.

"Watch me" came the reply.

"She can. She needs to see Gran" someone else said.

"But..."

The secretary's protests were cut short, as Chloe Gregson; Marina's granddaughter came in, leading Ethan and Rhys her 9 year old twins.

Following them was Todd, Marina's 6 year old great-grandson. His mother was her granddaughter Chanelle.

Someone else she recognised, as Angie Hunter came in behind her.

The sight of her, strangely did not comfort Marina.

"Gran thank God you're here. We went to the house, but Grandad said, you were here. We need to talk"

"I'll look after Ethan and Rhys" Angie said.

"They can show me those gold stars, they were talking about. Todd can read for me"

"Thanks Ang. Gran, can we go somewhere private"

Feeling unaccountably nervous, Marina followed her granddaughter out of the room.

They stopped in a corner of the corridor.

"Gran. There's no easy way to say this. Cameron was badly injured, when he was on duty last night"

Marina closed her eyes, and then opened them again, as if by doing so, she could make the words more bearable.

Her face was the colour of milk. Chloe was quite concerned, she might pass out, but she didn't. Her composure barely slipped at all.

"How bad?" she said finally.

"It's not looking good"

"Mum and Dad are both at the hospital. It's like World War III though. Mum said we should wait for news, before we told you, but Angie summoned Grandma Marissa, so Dad said you should be there too"

"Your Grandma's there? Oh and I've remembered why I still like Rueben"

"Yeah she and Angie have called a truce. Mum's spitting feathers, but after all Angie was JJ's wife, and if Grandma can stomach it"

"How is your Grandad getting there?" she asked.

At 84, Gabriel was no longer allowed to drive. He was quite resentful about it, but there wasn't anything he could do, because he just wasn't safe anymore.

"Callum and Connor are taking him. Chantelle and Chanelle will meet us there"

It didn't take very long, to get Marina excused the rest of the day off work.

She practically worked, when she wanted anyway. The head teacher told her to return, only when she was ready.

She collected her coat and handbag, with everyone staring at her. She felt like she was in a freak show, or something.

She parted company with her family, at their respective cars. She noticed that Angie, was driving Rueben's prized Ferrari.

He must be in a state, if he was letting someone else drive that.

She mentally kicked herself. Of course he was in a state.

He was immensely proud, of all his children, but Cameron was his first-born.

The one who faced the prospect of dying, every time he worked.

They were all anxious about him, and relieved every time he came home again safe and sound. Only this time he hadn't.

But there was no changing his mind, about how he wanted to earn his living.

He was 39 years old now after all, and perfectly capable of making his own decisions, about his career and his life in general.

Danielle had tried to hurt Rueben during the divorce, take him for everything he had.

She had tried to blacken his character, but one thing she couldn't take away, was the fact he was a decent father.

He had also never laid a finger on Danielle. Something that Marina knew, from Laurel Hunter was difficult for Rueben.

His family tree was littered, with wife-abusers. Rueben's own father, had been heavy with his fists.

Rueben and Darren Hunter had succeeded, in breaking the mould, as they had vowed to do.

Danielle had given Rueben plenty of provocation, but if he had ever been tempted, he had resisted.

Marina was naturally pleased about this, but she was well aware, just how difficult her middle child could be.

Rueben's stepmother of sorts, was a remarkable woman Marina thought, as she watched her across the car park.

She held herself with a dignity, which was entirely alien. She didn't look for the sympathy, some women might have.

Her husband had been, for want of a better phrase "a cheating bastard."

Marina's generation had been brought up, in a time when it was still a very shameful thing, to have to endure.

Not like nowadays. No one thought twice, before they did anything these days.

Angie had never once, begrudged Rueben anything even though he was evidence, that her husband had been unfaithful.

She took on Rueben and Belladonna's children and grandchildren, treating them like they really were her own.

The situation with Cameron, would be hurting her just as much as it was Marina or Marissa. Was this why

Marissa Hammond had called the truce, that Chloe had spoken of?

She pulled herself together reluctantly, and followed the scarlet Ferrari, which faithfully and considerately, kept in sight for her.

Chapter Twenty Two

DI Ivor Gunn and DS Arthur Jobb, were in Superintendent Oliver McCauley's office.

The Superintendent was furious at their incompetence.

The dressing down, had been the worst he had ever given them.

There were at least four dead bodies. Another had been found in the black van, when it was searched.

That body was officially unidentified. Her toe tag read "Jane Doe 25."

This meant she was the 25th unidentified female body, Byron Baron had dealt with this year.

The superintendent wasn't sure, that the body count from this operation, was not going to climb higher still.

Cameron Hammond, was still on the operating table fighting for his life. There had been no updates as yet.

There would have to be an investigation, into how the operation had been conducted.

Ivor might well be stripped of his rank.

Superintendent McCauley remembered Steven Potter, when he was a DS, facing a similar inquiry.

Why were the men of his squad, so bloody incapable these days?

The two men in front of him, stared at the floor, saying nothing.

"You may go"

The dismissal was curt and practised.

This man had spent 30 years, giving orders and seeing them obeyed.

"Well that could have been worse" Ivor said once they'd left the room, as fast as they could without actually running.

"Could have been a whole lot fucking better too" DS Jobb complained.

"Like how?" Ivor asked.

"Light duties. Weeks and weeks of catching up on paperwork, no one else can be arsed to write" Arthur replied.

Ivor grinned, but he had a feeling his Detective Sergeant was probably right.

He sighed deeply, as he sat down at his desk and stared blankly at his computer screen.

He was contemplating, what he should write in his report of the incident.

It would be the only opportunity, he would get to speak, as such in his own defence.

It had to be a truthful, but frankly awesome version, not a jumble of random, horrifying thoughts.

At the desk next to him, DS Jobb was doing the same, only his fingers were typing away, seemingly of their own accord, as though the report were a novel, he was composing.

Ivor stared out of the window, for a minute or two, and then began the mammoth task, of ordering his thoughts and scribbling them, into something capable of being followed.

As he worked on this assignment, a string of unpleasant images suppressed up until this moment, in time finally forced themselves back into his brain.

He wanted to put his head down, on the desk and howl. Instead, he forced his fingers, to start writing words.

Chapter Twenty Three

The hospital corridor outside Operating Theatre Number Two was packed.

But no one was talking much. There wasn't much point. No one had anything civil to say.

Marina Hemmingway had gone into the arms, her husband had held out to receive her, the moment the invitation had been offered.

They wouldn't normally have done this, but there was something warm and comforting about being held.

For his part, Gabriel just wanted to be doing something.

He stood next to his daughter, who sat stiffly on one of the chairs lining the wall.

She was alternately glaring at her ex-husband, and throwing dark looks at his stepmother.

Angie was doing a fine job, of ignoring these. She was far too used to them, to care.

Callum and Connor stood with their backs to the wall. Connor had one foot resting on the wall.

Chloe was smoothing out the hair, of one of the sleeping twins.

It was a reflexive, repetitive motion, almost as though she wasn't aware, she was making the movement.

If he had allowed himself to, he might have become hypnotised by it.

Instead, he looked at Chanelle. She was supporting a sleeping Todd on her lap.

Chantelle was staring fixedly at the floor. She hadn't taken her eyes off it, from the moment she'd arrived. It was almost as though she was afraid to.

As though by doing so, she would cause some change, to Cameron's condition.

Belladonna Richardson and her children were there. Shaun was staring off into space.

Stephanie was getting coffee for everyone. The others had various preoccupations, occupying their attention.

Edward Hunter was as they spoke, flying back from New York.

His wife would not accompany him, as she was still too annoyed, at his recent behaviour.

"What is taking your husband, and Doctor Benson so long" Danielle suddenly demanded, of Nurse Courtney Seabrook.

Courtney looked up startled, seemingly trying to think of a response.

"Life-saving stuff Danielle" Belladonna replied before Courtney could.

"It takes time you know" she added.

"They've been at it for hours" Danielle protested.

"He was quite badly injured Steven said"

Belladonna's tone was patient, striving for understanding.

The woman was in shock. She wasn't thinking straight. None of them were.

Bella had seen Steven. He had his arm, bound up in a sling.

Thomas Seabrook had been able, to remove the bullet without the need, for the before threatened operation.

Belladonna was immensely glad about this. The arm would be a mess, and wouldn't be any use for a long time, but given time and luck, the healing process would work its magic, and it would function properly again eventually.

Doctor's orders included rest, and to avoid all forms of stress.

Thomas had warned sternly, that worrying most definitely counted, in that category.

But Steven was ignoring this, and indulging in the activity anyway.

Belladonna knew, that Steven was anxious about Cameron.

Thomas Seabrook had rolled his eyes. He knew Steven too well, to think he would take his advice.

Thomas really was a handsome man, Belladonna thought as he disappeared, into the theatre to assist Adrian, with Cameron's operation.

Courtney had arrived sometime, after her husband had started his extra shift, meaning she had now not seen him, for several days in a row.

The theatre doors, had remained firmly closed ever since, Doctor Seabrook had gone through them, which was why Danielle and Rueben in particular, were so on edge.

Rueben had been for several walks. Being in the company of his ex-wife, was excruciating. He wished she would just disappear.

But that was never going to happen.

"Where are you going?" she demanded, when he next got up.

"For some fresh air"

"For a fag you mean?"

"Would you blame me, if I did?

"It's a filthy habit"

"It's been a stressful few years"

"You're never going to let us forget are you?"

"What's that supposed to mean?"

"Poor little Rueben. You lost your waste of space brother"

"What did you say?"

Angie could see the flame rising in Rueben. This was just like with Joseph.

"Rube walk away. Before you do something, we'll all regret" she said quietly.

Rueben nodded and began to obey.

"Don't you turn your back on me Rueben, and just who do you think you are? Danielle fumed.

This last part of the remark, had been directed at Angie.

"Me? I'm just one who has been, on the end of the Hunter streak of violence. You can't even see that you're pushing them, until the flame flares and boils over. It's been around since 1874 if not longer. It was rampant in my husband, dormant in my son and I'm damned, if I'll let it surface in my step-son" Angie replied.

"He's not your step-son. Your husband couldn't stand you. He preferred a stripper"

"Old news" Angie replied mildly.

Rueben slipped out. He went out into the hospital car park, found a convenient wall and sparked up.

"I always told Laurel, she should give up" his former mother-in-law had followed him.

"She never listened to you though, did she?" he said with a weak laugh.

"On some things, not on others. She always was stubborn. Look don't listen to Danielle. Don't let her provoke you" Marina's tone was gentle

"I know, it's just I feel so useless. She seems to forget he's my son too. This family has had a multi-million pound price, on its head since 1979, we just didn't know it then, like we do now. There's only so much tragedy, you can endure"

"When you get to my age, you've seen your fair share of it, believe me. You kind of get used to it. There comes a point, when you attend more funerals than you do weddings or Christenings. That's how you know, you've got old. It creeps up on you all of a sudden" Marina mused.

"When did you get so wise?" Rueben asked.

"A long acquaintance, with stubborn children" Marina replied.

"You have to know, how to handle them, because teachers don't have the time, or patience to deal with children" Marina grinned as she continued.

"Strange career choice for them then" Rueben observed.

Marina ignored this. So Rueben continued.

"It's Angie I feel sorry for. She's had so much pain and suffering. I wish I could take it away from her"

"You aren't God Rueben. Only he can do that, if he so wishes"

Marina looked thoughtful for a while. Rueben didn't break the silence. It was more comfortable this time.

"In my job, you get to know people. Laurel came to me, when she found out, she was expecting Charlie. She kept spouting on about abortion. I think she even went to the clinic, but, well put it this way, I was unsurprised when she came back still pregnant. And Natasha well, if anyone could cope with, how she was born, it was Laurel and your brother. You just have to take the rough with the smooth. You've had a lot of rough things happen, but hang in there Rube. Happiness will find you, you just have to have patience."

"Patience isn't a Hunter trait"

He didn't think she had heard him, but she eventually said

"So I'm learning. I knew your brother too remember"

She smiled and Rueben wondered why, Danielle had never smiled like that.

How did this woman, who was so jolly and liked by everyone, produce an offspring that was so bitter and twisted?

"We should get back, before they send out a search party" Marina suggested.

Perhaps her thoughts, had strayed to her daughter too.

Rueben's answering nod was reluctant.

When they returned to their own personal corridor, Adrian was just coming out of theatre.

He was dressed in his scrubs, and looked suitably gory.

"He's fighting. The next 48 hours will be critical. He's in Recovery, and will have to stay in the induced coma" Adrian explained.

He looked exhausted, but then he had been working for well over 24 hours.

Rueben and Danielle had called an uneasy truce, possibly Marina's doing.

She had got quite fed up, with Danielle's stinking attitude.

The atmosphere, was as thick as stodgy porridge, but passable as vaguely friendly.

It would do for now though. It wouldn't be forever. The recovery would be slow, if there was to be one.

Marina said that the bad vibes, wouldn't help.

They spent a rather long night, in his private room, holding his hand.

He looked a hideous sight, with tubes sticking out of his body.

Rueben wouldn't be at all surprised, if there wasn't an inch of his body, without a tube embedded in it.

At 9:00 the following morning, Rueben went home for a shower.

He called at Danielle's, to get her some fresh clothes.

She had kept the house, in the divorce. It had been part of the agreement, for an easy life. It was strange being back in that house.

By 10:30 he was back in his place, at Cameron's bedside. This is where he would remain, for several weeks.

Chapter Twenty-Four

Like Adrian Benson, Byron Baron pulled an all-night shift at the mortuary.

The Jane Doe now had a formal identity. They had used fingerprints and dental records, to identify her.

She was apparently Gabrielle Cullen. Byron had never seen so many bullets.

The hospital had couriered over the bullets, from Cameron. They all needed to be together.

The name Cullen seemed familiar. No, not because of the vampire family, in those old books and movies "The Twilight Saga" by Stephenie Meyer, but because he was sure he'd worked on a case, with corpses answering to that surname quite recently.

He would look out the details later.

While he worked Byron thought about "Donny", his husband.

Donatello was unhappy, that Byron wouldn't be home that evening, but what could Byron do about it?

It would just have been nice, after such a grim day at the office, piecing bodies back together in a multiple murder case, if there was someone there to give him a hug, at the end of it.

By the time he got home however, Donny would have left for his own job.

He and Donny had been talking, about having children recently.

They had put their names down, to be considered as adoptive parents.

If this turned out, not to be an option, they would go down the route, of finding a surrogate mother, willing to carry their child.

He couldn't see how, the adoption would be a problem though. Both he and Donny, had stable enough jobs.

Some might find Byron's job depressing, but Byron was used to this opinion.

He enjoyed his job. Someone had do to it.

Byron was a methodical man, and he catalogued things in perfect order.

His eyes stung with tiredness, and he knew he should take a break, before mistakes were made.

He decided to go, and get a coffee and a doughnut or a bagel.

He hadn't realized, just how hungry he was.

He said "Good Morning" to the security guard, at the reception desk, who just yawned at him.

He was particularly obnoxious.

Byron barely knew this particular security guard. He found it sad, that you needed a security guard, in a mortuary.

What was the world coming to? But people did steal bodies, and if they were unhappy, with a cause of a relatives' death, then they could sometimes become violent, like it was the pathologist's fault, that their relative had had a heart attack, or a brain haemorrhage.

Suicide tended to be difficult, because no one wants to hear, that their relative was so depressed, they took their own lives.

Murder is so much easier, to deal with.

Christmas came and went. Byron worked then too. Donny was visiting his mother. She didn't know, he was married to a man.

As far as she knew, Byron was just a friend he was renting his house with.

She was happier thinking this, so they left her with this impression.

She had been on holiday for the wedding.

Not a lot had changed, with the coming of the New Year. Cameron Hammond was still in hospital.

He was now out of Intensive Care, and complaining loudly. He was extremely bored by now.

He would be confined to a wheelchair, for a while after his discharge.

The hospital staff informed him, that he was doing well, but this wasn't much comfort.

He was on so many pain killers, and he was so high that he was hallucinating.

He had had to have more operations, much to his displeasure, but his parents at least were getting on better.

However, this was the only positive, he could find in the situation.

He would soon have as many scars, as Darren had had. He was redefining the term "walking wounded."

Chapter Twenty Five

The local Catholic priest, had a very busy month in January 2044.

He had to conduct more funerals, than he had ever had to officiate at before.

The first one had nothing, at all to do with the recent events, in Madeley Forest.

It was the funeral of Former DS Bruno Potter. He had died at the start of December.

He had had a chest infection, and had in effect suffocated, on his own bodily fluids.

It had been a horrific death. Steven didn't want to die like that.

Christie, Belladonna and Steven, had been by his bedside the whole near enough two days. it took him to die.

The funeral congregation was surprisingly large. None of this mattered, to Former DS Steven Potter.

He was just glad, that his father was now at peace.

He often wondered, whether he had found Joseph again. Had he wanted to?

Or were they ignoring each other? Chasing each other round with pitchforks, pulling each other's feathers out?

The service was moving and simple.

Bruno had never been a complicated man, and his send-off was accordingly fitting. The coffin was made of dark wood.

The next person to be buried, was David Appleby. His funeral was slightly more upbeat.

He'd only been in his 20s, when he died. It had more of a party atmosphere.

The music had a pop feel. Cameron Hammond attended, sitting at the back in his wheelchair, saying nothing and staring at the floor.

A few days later, Gabrielle Cullen got buried. Wayne made his one and only public appearance.

He was nervous, because he thought he might get recognized.

He didn't want any kind of publicity. But the event passed, without any incident at all. He knew he had failed, in his attempts to protect her.

She had sent him away, in the end. He had long since realized, she had planned it that way.

She had had no intention of surviving this. It was a last piece of fun, before she left.

She had been capable of the suicide, but she had wanted to be sure.

Everything she had done, had been leading to this end.

She hadn't wanted him to suffer, along with her. He was her oldest childhood friend.

But the fact remained, that he had made a promise to someone very special, and he had unintentionally broken that promise.

He hadn't looked after her at all. He had a sudden vision of hazel eyes, and black curls.

An identical pair of hazel eyes, on a full grown version minus the black curls, was all too knowing.

Wayne must admit the newcomer, looked good with wings sticking out, of the back of his leather jacket, though he would never have admitted that.

He also wore a red tie, knotted round his head like a bandana.

The vision stuck his finger up at Wayne, and then started doing air guitar, until Wayne grinned and shook his head.

Should an angel make such a rude gesture? But it seemed appropriate, coming from this angel at least. In death as he was in life.

Wayne knelt to pray, and a voice filled his head.

"It wasn't your fault, you did your best"

"But my best wasn't good enough"

"You know what a stubborn bitch she could be"

"Open the pearly gates for me"

"Oh we will. When it's your turn that is. All of us"

He sent one more question skywards.

"Yeah she did. No she didn't. Now no action man antics. I'll only push you back down"

In his head, the man smiled. The first smile, Wayne had seen on his face, in a while.

As they came out of the church, to go to the burial an unearthly voice floated back to him.

"My air guitar is perfect, thank you very much"

Wayne couldn't help it. He laughed out loud. It was a private joke, but he had shared plenty of these, with Gabrielle Cullen and her husband.

He would remember the better times with them, rather than these darkest of ones.

Wayne had finally found, a comfort that he had been seeking, and that had been eluding him, since news of Gabrielle's death, had reached his ears.

It had come through his mother, and that had hurt, but Gabrielle had no living family, to relay the news, so it had filtered slowly through the grapevine.

Gabrielle had written him a letter, which had arrived in the post.

Dear Wayne

By the time you read this, I shall have gone to a place, where you can't follow, so please don't try. I know you will be blaming yourself. If only this, if only that. Don't deny it. I know you far too well, and I wouldn't believe you anyway, so why bother?

Don't spend the rest of your life, seeking if onlys. It will not help you heal, and heal you must.

I have made my choice, and am happy with it. This whole mess you see, was a means to an end, but you will have worked this out. I truly am sorry, others had to suffer, along with me. It wasn't my intention.

You are a clever man, when you engage that brain of yours. You'll find it in your skull!

Only joking my friend. I go to seek happiness, and a peace I can't find on Earth, perhaps because it is does not exist there. Keep reading Oedipus and the legends of Thebes, and think of me as you do so.

Remember this; your heart, is made of the purest, rarest gold, anyone will ever find.

I am proud, to have been able, to call you my best friend.

Until the day we meet again, if you have need of me, look inside yourself. You will find us all, in the region of your heart.

If I don't stop writing this letter, I never shall.

All my love

Your friend (If I may sign myself as such still)

Gabrielle (Gabby)

Once home again, and alone in his study, he took out this letter, and re-read it, and this time no tears fell, to blotch the paper.

He was all out of tears. The well had dried. He had reached the understanding; she had always meant him to.

He could live with that

Chapter Twenty-Six

The day of Rose-Anna Rabin's funeral, dawned frosty. It was about to snow, by the looks of it.

Now though, it was bucketing down with rain.

Heidi was sat in her daughter's bedroom, at 5:00 in the morning.

She was already dressed in black. She hadn't slept at all, the previous evening and neither had Eddie.

They kept disturbing each other, so they had got up and done practical things, to get things ready for the funeral.

As a result, they were ready hours before, they needed to be.

So this left Heidi, with time to fill, which wasn't a good thing these days.

She hadn't been to work, since Rose's death either.

She had been in Rose-Anna's room every day, since her death, but hadn't changed a thing in there.

She probably never would. Rose-Anna had left it that way.

Even the dirty plates, cups and glasses, were still scattered, where Rose had casually dumped them.

She thought back to Christmas. It had been hell. Rose's presents bought back in November, had lain there in a pile, mocking them.

Eventually, she had been unable to stand it, and had ripped them open, like a demon possessed.

At meal times, she still set that extra place, because not to do so, felt like an acknowledgement, and she was not yet ready, to acknowledge.

Heidi's eyes were red, with lack of sleep. She hadn't cried yet. Her grief was inexpressible through tears.

Eddie was rather worried about her. He'd made an appointment for her, to see the doctor.

The doctor had suggested a counsellor, and she had an appointment with her, on Monday next week.

Heidi wasn't sure, whether she would go to the appointment.

But there was no need, to tell Eddie this.

How could she explain, that though immediate justice had been dispensed, i.e. her daughter's murderer had himself received the death penalty, within half an hour, that it wasn't enough?

She needed to see justice done, in a court of law, but could she have sat through a trial, day in day out?

She wasn't sure, so perhaps it was cleaner, this way. But Rose had left her legacy.

Elizabeth-Ellen, had never got on overly well with Rose-Anna, but she was devastated.

She visited her parents every day now, something that never used to happen before.

This was the only good thing, which had come out of Rose's death.

Lizzie had postponed her wedding.

She had announced that she couldn't get married, with Rose-Anna's absence so fresh.

It would take place in the July, instead of February. She had found another bridesmaid.

At 10:30, Eddie knocked on the door, of Rose-Anna's room.

"Heidi, we need to go" he said gently.

They were getting on better, these days too. She nodded, but said nothing.

The funeral cars had arrived, and the hearse was standing there.

They had hired a horse and carriage hearse, rather than a car.

Rose had always liked horses. They were perfectly well behaved animals. The cars would follow behind.

Rose had wanted a horse, since she was four years old, but had never got round, to actually owning one.

Instead, she had had riding lessons. They could do this for her now though.

Heidi had gone to the funeral home, and to its chapel of rest, to view Rose-Anna's body.

She wished she hadn't. Eddie had advised her not to go.

She had ignored him, but wished now that she had listened to him.

She was impressed that they had managed, to hide the wound left in her head, by the murdering bullet.

She wasn't sure, she would have been able to stomach seeing that. Even so it was still a rather grim experience.

Heidi looked pointedly away, from the hearse. Bouquets of flowers adorned the coffin. The coffin was made of pine.

Looking at that coffin, was just a little too much. She nearly cried right there and then, and they hadn't even started the service yet.

Eddie slipped a supporting yet invisible hand, round her waist.

He was watching her like a hawk, because he was waiting for her to break. Her grief was poisonous.

She needed to cry, because it would be a relief and a release, but she refused to.

It was eating away at her inside. Anyone could see this.

The journey to the church, was sombre and therefore boring.

Rose-Anna would have found this ridiculous, and would have rolled her eyes, at the need to follow tradition.

The church was packed with people. All of Rose-Anna's friends, of which she had plenty turned out.

The hymns were "The Day You Gave Us Lord Has Ended" and "Abide with Me."

Nobody present would ever, be able to listen to those hymns again. The association would be too much, to bear.

Eddie shuddered at the burial, when the earth was thrown in.

Rose had always hated being underground, and not having an escape route. He didn't suppose, it would bother her now, but still.

He kept a firm hold on Heidi's waist. She looked as though, she was on the verge, of throwing herself into the grave with the coffin.

He had seen it on TV, and it was never pleasant.

The wake was held at the local pub.

Everyone got drunk, but Rose wouldn't have begrudged anyone a drink.

There were plenty of times, when she had herself, with hilarious consequences. They all swapped memories of Rose.

However three hours later, when it was all over, everything seemed to go a little flat.

Life was now changed forever. Organising a funeral had made time pass, but now they had so much time to fill.

What were they going to do now?

Chapter Twenty Seven

Cameron Hammond was in hospital, until the start of March.

Danielle threw him a huge party to celebrate his discharge. But Cameron wasn't in the mood to be celebrating.

So many people had died, that day in December in Madeley Forest.

He felt he would never be able, to go to that place again.

Steven's arm was set free, from its sling in February. Adrian Benson gave him a long lecture, on dangerous and life-threatening activities.

"Will you stop being a worrywart?" Steven replied.

"I don't want to be sewing you back together, anytime soon" Adrian retorted.

"Can't promise anything, life might get boring if we're not careful" Steven retorted back.

"And anyway, we all have an expiry date. You can't keep defying God forever Ade, skilled doctor and surgeon you might be, but He will always win any battle between you, maybe not today or tomorrow, but ultimately."

Adrian grunted something unintelligible, perhaps about Steven missing some kind of point.

He quite often did.

"Oh lighten up Doc. Life's far too fucking short. I thought you'd know that, working where you do"

He playfully jabbed Adrian in the arm.

"Ow, watch it. These arms are delicate. It might have escaped your notice, but they are connected to my hands" Adrian complained with a wink.

"Oh is that a fact?"

"A scientifically proven one"

Adrian stuck his tongue out.

"I've had these hands insured for millions I have"

"Adrian, anorak you might be with your medical science and obsession with biology, but even you aren't quite sad enough, to insure your own hands

"No, I'll give you that. Hey, watch who you're calling an anorak"

"Admit it, you're such a geek Ade"

"I so am not"

"You so are"

"Don't make me come back over there, Steven Bruno Potter"

"Now I'm scared" Steven pretended to tremble.

"You should be. I might get Paul, to make a case for slander"

"Tell you what. We'll have a game of Poker. If I win you are officially a geek, if you win, I'll apologize and never slander you, so outrageously ever again, and the loser buys the winner a drink, to acknowledge the winner's proven, much superior card playing skills?"

"Deal" Adrian replied.

"Strip Poker Ade"

"Still a deal"

Adrian held out his hand, and they spit shook on it, like the four of them, had as children. It signified a solemn and binding contract.

"Now get out of here. I've got other patients to see"

On 17th March 2044, Steven, Adrian, Paul and Rueben all stood around Laurel and Darren Hunter's grave.

They did this every year. It had become tradition, and they stuck to it like glue.

It was almost as though, if they didn't do this, the world might fly apart.

The lettering on the grave, was starting to peel a little. The weather had taken its toll on it.

They would need to get it re-done, at some point.

Several hundreds of yards away, were the fresh earth of three new graves.

They had all been buried next to each other, David, Gabrielle and Rose-Anna.

Gabrielle's name had been engraved below that, of her husband and another name, that of a person with hazel eyes and black curls.

Chapter Twenty Eight

Epilogue

Time passed, as time must always pass, regardless of how much we wish it wouldn't.

Elizabeth-Ellen Rabin, got married in the July of 2044, as planned.

She tried to enjoy herself, but didn't quite manage to. She had to admit, it wasn't quite the same, without her little sister there.

The girl she had chosen, as replacement bridesmaid was a great friend, but she wasn't Rose.

She hadn't grown up pulling Lizzie's hair; she hadn't broken her parents' best ornaments, and blamed Lizzie for it.

She didn't know Lizzie like a sister, because only a true sister can do that, or has the right to do so.

Lizzie knew, she had taken Rose for granted, or at least the fact, that she would always be there, but now of course she wasn't.

Lizzie had had a baby girl, in the May following her sister's death, ironically on what would have been Rose-Anna's 24th birthday, 13th May.

That was the news, she had wanted to deliver that day, when she saw Rose, for what turned out to be the last time.

She had taken the fact, that the baby shared a birthday, with her aunt as a sign, and put a plan into action, she had been thinking about for a while.

She had named her new daughter Rose.

Not Rose-Anna, her sister had hated the name, so much as one form, she was adamant about this, just plain "Rose."

She had been a little nervous, about telling her parents this, but they seemed to have no objection to it.

She was hoping that baby Rose's presence, in their lives might have a healing effect, in their lives and in the three months since the child's birth, she had started to see some healing start.

She knew nothing, would ever heal it completely, but she was hopeful, it would stop festering, dripping pus and then bursting open, and bleeding afresh when you least expected it to.

Doctor Adrian Benson, and Former DS Steven Potter got round to having their bet, and Poker game sometime in April.

Some days later, Steven received the following communication.

Dear Sir

Doctor Adrian Benson has instructed me, to inform you that he is not a geek, anorak or anything else, as proven by your legally binding contract, the means of which were previously agreed between you.

Should you ever imply, such a slanderous thing again, then it will be taken, as before mentioned slander, and in event of such a slight, on my client's character, then I have been instructed, to start immediate legal proceedings against you.
Yours sincerely

P.T Granger

Senior Partner of Granger, Hadley & Granger Solicitors at Law.

Steven read this in disbelief, and then he was laughing. Laughing so much, he was rolling on the floor.

Kayla looking up from a letter, she was writing looked at him in some alarm.

She was clearly wondering, if she should summon a doctor, or whether it was too late, and the men in white coats, armed with a straitjacket were called for.

"What's up with you?" she asked.

"Nothing. Just Adrian and Paul" Steven choked.

"Ri...ii...ght" Kayla drew out the one-word response, eyebrows raised.

Obviously deciding, she didn't want to know, she went back to writing the novel, she called a letter, reaching the end of the page, and starting a fresh one.

Steven was only brought round, from his fit of laughter, snorting and coughing, when Lance obviously deciding that his daddy, was some kind of dangerous lunatic, intervened by expertly throwing a wooden alphabet block, at his father's head.

The pain soon sobered Steven up.

"Oi, you little monster" he howled.

Elizabeth-Ellen pushed the pram, through the gates of the cemetery.

It was a wonderful August day, and her daughter's brown hair, was covered by a hat.

She found the now familiar black headstone. She was glad now, that they had resisted the urge, to go for white.

She read the inscription she knew by heart, but she read it anyway.

In Loving Memory of

Rose-Anna Rabin

13th May 2020-5th December 2043

A much loved daughter, sister and aunt

Rose had often expressed the opinion, that gravestones were hypocritical, in their inscriptions.

"All they really want to say is, I hated the old bugger. What it really should say is....

In Indifferent Memory of Joe Average.
He was a tight-fisted git, who'd walk across the road to pick up a one pence piece, and I hated the moaning old shit, because I gave up years nursing him, and was he grateful, was he fuck?"

Elizabeth-Ellen remembered this, as she bent to remove the dead flowers, from the pots and split the new bunch she'd bought.

There was a man at the next grave. He had a flat cap, rather like a Grandad might wear, pulled over his eyes, though he couldn't be more than 26, 27 at oldest.

"Morning" Elizabeth greeted him politely.

"Morning" Wayne responded.

He lingered to watch, as the young woman arranged her flowers, bought a young girl, perhaps her daughter to the graveside. She chatted nonsense.

The child had eyes the colour of chocolate. He was speared with them.

He remembered meeting Rose-Anna Rabin once, on a quick trip to her branch, in his role as Area Manager.

The meeting had been so brief, he wasn't sure had he met her, while she was being held hostage, in that disgusting cellar, she would have recognised him.

When the young woman left, babbling to the child about visiting Grandma and Grandad, Wayne watched her out of sight. Then he stepped across the divide.

He stood in front of Rose-Anna's gravestone.

"I'm sorry. I kept telling myself, that if I kept denying it she wouldn't go through with the idea. She was backing out you know. She wasn't always like that. The last few months, she just lost too much, reached her snapping point"

He laid a hand, on the top of the headstone.

"But if I had intervened, you wouldn't be where you are now. I have to learn to live, with that knowledge. Denial is a horrible thing. It makes liars of the best people. Friends become enemies. Denial is the best weapon in war. It splits people down the middle. Innocent victims of denial, realize what they've done, but only when it is far too late, to make amends."

As he walked away, his communion with the dead done, he was sure he saw several ghostly figures.

A young woman in her early 20s, with dyed tomato red hair and chocolate eyes.

She simply nodded at him and smiled.

A man with greying blonde hair, had his arm round the transparent waist of his wife.

Her hair was auburn, also greying at the edges.

He noticed them, because of the contrast between them. His eyes a sapphire blue and hers, a vivid startling emerald green.

A little further off, was a young woman that was very familiar to him.

She was holding hands, and walking with a man who had blonde hair and hazel eyes.

He was supporting her, so she didn't fall, just as he used to do.

Neither appeared to notice Wayne. A rustle caught his ears.

A child covered his eyes. His black hair, curled tightly to his head.

If he took his hands away, they would be a shade of hazel.

Wayne debated, but before he could make a decision, two other children, came up to the child and pushed him playfully over.

He spluttered with shock, but quickly recovered chasing the two children, into the bushes.

When they emerged, the small boy with blonde hair and sapphire blue eyes, who could only be four, had leaves sticking in his hair.

The girl who was possibly 2 years old, perhaps younger giggled.

Her auburn hair, was standing on end, but her emerald eyes shone with delight.

The woman walking with her husband, called to them and they ran to her instantly.

The blonde-haired boy, wriggled and squirmed away from his mother, as she vigorously brushed leaves out of his hair.

He was the spitting image of his father. Wayne decided he had seen enough.

He vaulted the gate, and began to walk down the lane beyond.

He reflected that you could lay ghosts to rest, all you wanted, but ghosts were restless.

They were never truly at rest; they were just somewhere else, waiting for when it was your time, to join them. He could live with that knowledge.

"Until we meet again" he said to thin air.

And he could have sworn, that there were three peals of ghostly laughter, two were definitely adult, but one was almost certainly childish.

The End

Printed in Great Britain
by Amazon

65417325R00106